Read ALL the CAT WHO mysteries!

THE CAT WHO COULD READ BACKWARDS: The world of modern art is a mystery to many—but for Jim Qwilleran and Koko it's a mystery of another sort . . .

THE CAT WHO ATE DANISH MODERN: Qwill isn't thrilled about covering interior design for *The Daily Fluxion.* Little does he know that a murderer has designs on a woman featured in one of his stories . . .

THE CAT WHO TURNED ON AND OFF: Qwill and Koko are joined by Yum Yum as they try to solve a murder in an antique shop . . .

THE CAT WHO SAW RED: Qwill starts his diet—*and* a new gourmet column for the *Fluxion.* It isn't easy—but it's not as hard as solving a murder case!

THE CAT WHO PLAYED BRAHMS: Fishing at a secluded cabin, Qwill hooks on to a mystery—and Koko develops a strange fondness for classical music . . .

THE CAT WHO PLAYED POST OFFICE: Koko and Yum Yum turn into fat cats when Qwill inherits millions. But amid the caviar and champagne, Koko starts sniffing clues to a murder!

THE CAT WHO HAD 14 TALES: A delightful collection of feline mystery fiction from the creator of Koko and Yum Yum!

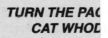

TURN THE PAG
CAT WHO

D0019953

THE CAT WHO KNEW SHAKESPEARE: The local newspaper publisher has perished in an accident—or is it murder? That is the question . . .

THE CAT WHO SNIFFED GLUE: After a banker and his wife are killed, Koko develops an odd appetite for glue. To solve the case, Qwill has to figure out why . . .

THE CAT WHO WENT UNDERGROUND: Qwill and the cats head for their Moose County cabin for a relaxing summer—but when a handyman disappears, Koko must dig up the motive for a sinister crime . . .

THE CAT WHO TALKED TO GHOSTS: Qwill and Koko try to solve a haunting mystery in a historic farmhouse.

THE CAT WHO LIVED HIGH: An art dealer was killed in Qwill's high-rise apartment—and he and the cats reach new heights in detection as they find out whodunit . . .

THE CAT WHO KNEW A CARDINAL: The director of the local Shakespeare production dies in Qwill's orchard—and the stage is set for a puzzling mystery!

THE CAT WHO MOVED A MOUNTAIN: Qwill has a new home in the scenic Potato Mountains. But when a dispute between residents and developers boils over into murder, he has to keep his eyes open to find the culprit!

THE CAT WHO WASN'T THERE: Qwill's on his way to Scotland—to solve another purr-plexing mystery!

THE CAT WHO WENT INTO THE CLOSET: Qwill's moved into a mansion . . . with fifty closets for Koko to investigate! But among the junk, Koko finds a clue—and Qwill's unearthing some surprising skeletons . . .

THE CAT WHO CAME TO BREAKFAST: Peaceful Breakfast Island is turned upside-down by controversy—and murder. Qwill and the cats must find out whodunit . . .

THE CAT WHO BLEW THE WHISTLE: An old steam locomotive has been restored, causing excitement in Moose County. But a murder brings the fun to a screeching halt—and Qwill and Koko are tracking down the culprit . . .

THE CAT WHO SAID CHEESE: The Great Food Explo brings lots of delicious activity to Moose County—as well as a stew of gossip, mystery, and murder . . .

THE CAT WHO TAILED A THIEF: A rash of petty thievery in Pickax puts Qwill and Koko on a killer's elusive trail . . .

THE CAT WHO SANG FOR THE BIRDS: Qwilleran is looking forward to the peaceful beauty of a Moose County spring. Instead, he gets a chorus of noisy birds, a chain of mysterious events—and a bird-calling cat whose fancy has turned to crimesolving . . .

THE CAT WHO SAW STARS: UFOS in Mooseville? With the help of his own little aliens, Qwill investigates the rumors that are flying—but the search for intelligent life turns into a search for a killer . . .

THE CAT WHO ROBBED A BANK
Available in hardcover from G. P. Putnam's Sons

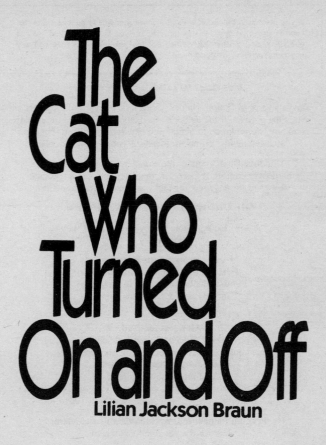

The Cat Who Turned On and Off

Lilian Jackson Braun

JOVE BOOKS, NEW YORK

This is a work of fiction. Names, characters, places, and incidents are either the product of the author's imagination or are used fictitiously, and any resemblance to actual persons, living or dead, business establishments, events, or locales is entirely coincidental.

This Jove Book contains the complete text of the original hardcover edition. It has been completely reset in a typeface designed for easy reading and was printed from new film.

THE CAT WHO TURNED ON AND OFF

A Jove Book / published by arrangement with the author

PRINTING HISTORY
E. P. Dutton edition published 1968
Published simultaneously in Canada by
Clarke, Irwin & Company Limited
Jove edition / December 1986

The Penguin Putnam Inc. World Wide Web site address is
http://www.penguinputnam.com

ISBN: 0-515-08794-7

A JOVE BOOK®
Jove Books are published by
The Berkley Publishing Group, a division of Penguin Putnam Inc.,
375 Hudson Street, New York, New York 10014.
JOVE and the "J" design are trademarks
belonging to Penguin Putnam Inc.

PRINTED IN THE UNITED STATES OF AMERICA

35   34   33   32   31   30   29

ONE

In December the weather declared war. First it bombarded the city with ice storms, then strafed it with freezing winds. Now it was snowing belligerently. A blizzard whipped down Canard Street, past the Press Club, as if it had a particular grudge against newspapermen. With malicious accuracy the largest flakes zeroed in to make cold wet landings on the neck of the man who was hailing a taxi in front of the club.

He turned up the collar of his tweed overcoat—awkwardly, with one hand—and tried to jam his porkpie hat closer to his ears. His left hand was plunged deep in his coat pocket and held stiffly there. Otherwise there was nothing remarkable about the man except the luxuriance of his moustache—and his sobriety. It was after midnight; it was nine days before Christmas; and the man coming out of the Press Club bar was sober.

When a cab pulled to the curb, he eased himself carefully into the back seat, keeping his left hand in his pocket, and gave the driver the name of a third-rate hotel.

"Medford Manor? Let's see, I can take Zwinger Street and the expressway," the cabbie said hopefully as he threw the flag on the meter, "or I can take Center Boulevard."

"Zwinger," said the passenger. He usually took the Boulevard route, which was cheaper, but Zwinger was faster.

"You a newspaperman?" the driver asked, turning and giving his fare a knowing grin.

The passenger mumbled an affirmative.

"I figured. I knew you couldn't be one of them publicity types that hang around the Press Club. I mean, I can tell by the way you dress. I don't mean newspapermen are slobs or anything like that, but they're—well *you* know! I pick 'em up in front of the Press Club all the time. Not very big tippers, but good guys, and you never know you're gonna need a friend at the paper. Right?" He turned and flashed a conspiratorial grin at the back seat.

"Watch it!" snapped the passenger as the cab

veered toward a drunk staggering across Zwinger Street.

"You with the *Daily Fluxion* or the *Morning Rampage*?"

"*Fluxion.*"

The cab stopped for a red light, and the driver stared at his passenger. "I've seen your picture in the paper. The moustache, I mean. You get a by-line?"

The man in the back seat nodded.

They were in a blighted area now. Cheap lodgings and bars occupied old town houses that had once been the homes of the city's elite.

"Lock your door," the driver advised. "You wouldn't believe the scum that drifts around this street after dark. Drunks, hopheads, cruisers, you-name-it. Used to be a ritzy neighborhood. Now they call it Junktown."

"Junktown?" repeated the passenger with his first show of interest in the conversation.

"You a newspaper guy and you never heard of Junktown?"

"I'm a—I'm fairly new in the city." The passenger smoothed his moustache with his right hand.

His left was still in his pocket when he got out of the cab on the other side of town. Entering the deserted lobby of the Medford Manor, he walked hurriedly past the registration desk, where the elderly clerk sat dozing at the switchboard. In the elevator he found an aged bellhop slumped on a stool, snoring softly. The man flicked a switch and pressed a lever, taking the car and its sleeping occupant to the sixth floor.

Then he strode down the corridor to room 606. With his right hand he found a key in his trouser pocket, unlocked the door, and stepped inside the room. He closed the door gently before switching on the light. Then he stood and listened. He moved his head slowly from side to side, examining the room: the double bed, the armchair, the cluttered dresser, the closet door standing ajar.

"All right, you guys," he said. "Come on out!"

Slowly and cautiously he withdrew his left hand from his pocket.

"I know you're here. Come on out!"

There was a creaking of bedsprings and a grunt, followed by a sharp ripping sound and two soft thuds on the floor. Between the limp fringes of the cotton bedspread there appeared two heads.

"You crazy nuts! You were inside the bedsprings again!"

They squeezed out from under the bed—two Siamese cats. First there were two brown heads, one more wedge-shaped than the other; then two pale fawn bodies, one daintier than the other; then two brown silky tails, one with a kink in the tip.

The man held out his left hand, exhibiting a soggy mass in a paper napkin. "See what I brought you? Turkey from the Press Club."

Two black velvet noses sniffed the air, two sets of whiskers twitched, and both cats howled in unison.

"Shhh! The old gal next door will have you arrested."

The man started cutting up the turkey with a

pocket knife, while they paced the room in ecstatic figure eights, waving their tails and howling a discordant duet.

"Quiet!"

They howled louder.

"I don't know why I do this for you heathens. It's against the rules—sneaking takeouts from the Press Club buffet. Not to mention the mess! I've got a pocketful of gravy."

They drowned out his voice with their clamor.

"Will you guys shut up?"

The telephone rang.

"See? I told you so!"

The man hurriedly placed a glass ashtray full of turkey on the floor and went to the telephone.

"Mr. Qwilleran," said the quavering voice of the desk clerk, "sorry to call you again, but Mrs. Mason in 604 says your cats—"

"Sorry. They were hungry. They're quiet now."

"If—if—if you don't mind taking an inside room, 619 is vacant, and you could ask the day clerk tomorrow—"

"It won't be necessary. We're moving out as soon as I find an apartment."

"I hope you're not offended, Mr. Qwilleran. The manager—"

"No offense, Mr. McIldoony. A hotel room is no place for cats. We'll be out before Christmas . . . I hope," he added softly, surveying the bleak room.

He had lived in better places when he was young and successful and well-known and married. Much had happened since his days as a crime reporter in New York. Now, considering his backlog of debts and the wage scale on a Midwestern newspaper, the Medford Manor was the best he could afford. Qwilleran's only luxury was a pair of roommates whose expensive tastes he was inclined to indulge.

The cats were quiet now. The larger one was gobbling turkey with head down and tail up, its tip waving in the slow rhythm of rapture. The little female, sitting a few inches apart, was respectfully waiting her turn.

Qwilleran took off his coat and tie and crawled under the bed to thumbtack the torn ticking to the wooden frame of the box spring. There had been a small rip when he moved into the hotel two weeks ago, and it had steadily enlarged. He had composed a pseudoserious essay on the subject for the feature page of the *Daily Fluxion*.

"Any small aperture is challenging to the feline sensibility," he had written. "For a cat it is a matter of honor to enlarge the opening and squeeze through."

After repairing the spring, Qwilleran groped in his coat pocket for his pipe and tobacco and withdrew a handful of envelopes. The first, postmarked Connecticut, was still sealed and unread, but he knew what it contained—another graceless hint for money.

The second—a note written in brown ink with feminine flourishes—he had read several times. Regretfully she was canceling their date for Christmas Eve. With tact so delicate that it was painful she was explaining that this other man—this engineer—it was all so sudden—Qwill would understand.

Qwilleran twisted the note into a bowknot before dropping it in the wastebasket. He had half expected this news. She was young, and the Qwilleran moustache and temples were graying noticeably. It was a disappointment, nevertheless. Now he had no date for the Christmas Eve party at the Press Club—the only Christmas celebration he expected to have.

The third communication was a memo from the managing editor, reminding staffers of the annual writing competition. Besides $3,000 in cash prizes there would be twenty-five frozen turkeys for honorable mentions, donated by Cybernetic Poultry Farms, Inc.

"Who will expect to be loved, cherished, and publicized by *Fluxion* writers till death do us part," said Qwilleran, aloud.

"Yow," said Koko between licks, as he washed his face.

The little female was now taking her turn at the turkey; Koko always left half the food for her—or a good 40 percent.

Qwilleran stroked Koko's fur, soft as ermine, and marveled at its shading—from pale fawn to seal brown—one of nature's more spectacular successes. Then he lighted his pipe and slouched in the armchair with his feet on the bed. He could use one of those cash prizes. He could send a couple of hundred to Connecticut and then start buying furniture. If he had his own furniture, it would be easier to find lodgings that accepted pets.

There was still time to write something prizeworthy and get it published before the December 31 deadline, and the feature editor was desperate for Christmas material. Arch Riker had called a meeting of the feature staff, saying, "Can't you guys come up with some ideas?" Without much hope he had searched the faces of the assembled staffers: the paunchy columnists, the cadaverous critics, Qwilleran on general assignment, and the specialist who handled travel, hobbies, aviation, real estate, and gardening. They had all stared back at the editor with the blank gaze of veterans who had reported on too many Yuletides.

Qwilleran noticed Koko watching him closely. "To win a prize," he told the cat, "you've got to have a gimmick."

"Yow," said Koko. He jumped to the bed and looked at the man with sympathetically blinking eyes. They were sapphire blue in bright light, but in the lamplit hotel room they were large circles of black onyx with flashes of diamond or ruby.

"What I need is an idea that's spectacular but not cheap." Qwilleran was frowning and jabbing his moustache with his pipestem. He was thinking irritably about the *Fluxion*'s Jack Jaunti, a young smart-aleck in the Sunday Department who had taken a job as Percival Duxbury's valet, incognito, in order to write an inside story on the richest man in town. The stunt had won no friends among the city's First Families, but it had increased circulation for two weeks, and the rumor was that Jaunti would walk off with first prize. Qwilleran resented juveniles who substituted nerve for ability.

"Why, that guy can't even spell," he said to his attentive audience of one.

Koko went on blinking. He looked sleepy.

The female cat was on the prowl, searching for playthings. She rose on her hind legs to examine the contents of the wastebasket and hauled out a twist of paper about the size of a mouse. She brought it to Qwilleran in her teeth and dropped it—the letter written in brown ink—on his lap.

"Thanks, but I've read it," he said. "Don't rub it in." He groped in the drawer of the nightstand, found a rubber mouse and tossed it across the room. She bounded after it, sniffed it, arched her back and returned to the wastebasket, this time extracting a crumpled paper handkerchief, which she presented to the man in the armchair.

"Why do you fool around with junk?" he said. "You've got nice toys."

Junk! Qwilleran experienced a prickling sensation in the roots of his moustache, and a warmth spread over his face.

"Junktown!" he said to Koko. "Christmas in Junktown! I could write a heartbreaker." He came out of his slouch and slapped the arms of the chair. "And it might get me out of this damned rut!"

His job in the Feature Department was considered a comfortable berth for a man over forty-five, but interviewing artists, interior decorators and Japanese flower arrangers was not Qwilleran's idea of newspapering. He longed to be writing about con men, jewel thieves, and dope peddlers.

Christmas in Junktown! He had done Skid Row assignments in the past, and he knew how to proceed: quit shaving—pick up some ratty clothes—get to know the people in the dives and on the street—and then listen. The trick would be to make the series compassionate, relating the personal tragedies behind society's outcasts, plucking the heartstrings.

"Koko," he said, "by Christmas Eve there won't be a dry eye in town!"

Koko was watching Qwilleran's face and blinking. The cat spoke in a low voice, but with a sense of urgency.

"What's on your mind?" Qwilleran asked. He knew the water dish was freshly filled. He knew the sandbox in the bathroom was clean.

Koko stood up and walked across the bed. He rubbed the side of his jaw against the footboard, then looked at Qwilleran over his shoulder. He rubbed the other side of his jaw, and his fangs clicked against the metal finial of the bedpost.

"You want something? What is it you want?"

The cat gave a sleepy yowl and jumped to the top edge of the footboard, balancing like a tightrope walker. He walked its length and then, with forepaws against the wall, stretched his neck and scraped his jaw against the light switch. It clicked, and the light went out. Murmuring little noises of satisfaction, Koko made himself a nest on the bed and curled up for sleep.

TWO

"Christmas in Junktown!" Qwilleran said to the feature editor. "How does that grab you?"

Arch Riker was sitting at his desk, browsing through the Friday morning mail and tossing most of it over his shoulder in the direction of a large wire bin.

Qwilleran perched on the corner of the editor's desk and waited for his old friend's reaction, knowing there would be no visible clue. Riker's face had the composure of a seasoned deskman, registering no surprise, no enthusiasm, no rejection.

"Junktown?" Riker murmured. "It might have possibilities. How would you approach it?"

"Hang around Zwinger Street, mix with the characters there, get them to talk."

The editor leaned back in his chair and clasped his hands behind his head. "Okay, go ahead."

"It's a hot subject, and I can give it a lot of heart."

Heart was the current password at the *Daily Fluxion*. In frequent memos from the managing editor, staff writers were reminded to put heart into everything including the weather report.

Riker nodded. "That'll make the boss happy. And it should get a lot of readership. My wife will like it. She's a junker."

He said it calmly, and Qwilleran was shocked. "Rosie? You mean—"

Riker was rocking contentedly in his swivel chair. "She got hooked a couple of years ago, and it's been keeping me poor ever since."

Qwilleran stroked his moustache to hide his dismay. He had known Rosie years ago when he and Arch were cub reporters in Chicago. Gently he asked, "When—how did this happen, Arch?"

"She went to Junktown with some gal friends one day and got involved. I'm beginning to get interested myself. Just paid twenty-eight dollars for an old tea canister in painted tin. Tin is what I go for—tin boxes, tin lanterns—"

Qwilleran stammered, "What—what—what are you talking about?"

"Junk. Antiques. What are *you* talking about?"

"Hell, I'm talking about narcotics!"

"I said we were junkers, not junkies!" Arch said. "Junktown, for your information, is the place with all the antique shops."

"The cabdriver said it was a hangout for hopheads."

"Well, you know how cabdrivers are. Sure, it's a declining neighborhood, and the riffraff may come out after dark, but during the day it's full of respectable junkpickers like Rosie and her friends. Didn't your ex-wife ever take you junking?"

"She dragged me to an antique show in New York once, but I hate antiques."

"Too bad," said Arch. "Christmas in Junktown sounds like a good idea, but you'd have to stick to antiques. The boss would never go for the narcotics angle."

"Why not? It would make a poignant Christmas story."

Riker shook his head. "The advertisers would object. Readers spend less freely when their complacency is disturbed."

Qwilleran snorted his disdain.

"Why don't you go ahead, Qwill, and do a Christmas series on antiquing?"

"I hate antiques, I told you."

"You'll change your mind when you get to Junktown. You'll be hooked like the rest of us."

"Want to bet?"

Arch took out his wallet and extracted a small

yellow card. "Here's a directory of the Junktown dealers. Let me have it back."

Qwilleran glanced at some of the names: Ann's 'Tiques, Sorta Camp, The Three Weird Sisters, the Junque Trunque. His stomach rebelled. "Look, Arch, I wanted to write something for the contest—something with guts! What can I do with antiques? I'd be lucky if I tied for the twenty-fifth frozen turkey."

"You might be surprised! Junktown is full of kooks, and there's an auction this afternoon."

"I can't stand auctions."

"This should be a good one. The dealer was killed a couple of months ago, and they're liquidating his entire stock."

"Auctions are the world's biggest bore, if you want my opinion."

"A lot of the dealers in Junktown are single girls—divorcees—widows. That's something you should appreciate. Look, you donkey, why do I have to give you a big selling on this boondoggle? It's an assignment. Get busy."

Qwilleran gritted his teeth. "All right. Give me a taxi voucher. Round trip!"

He took time to have his hair trimmed and his moustache pruned—his standard procedure before tackling a new beat, although he had intended to postpone this nicety until Christmas. Then he hailed a cab and rode out Zwinger Street, not without misgivings.

Downtown it was a boulevard of new office

buildings, medical clinics, and fashionable apartment houses. Then it ran through a snow-covered
wasteland where a former slum had been cleared.
Farther out there were several blocks of old buildings with boarded windows, awaiting demolition.
Beyond that was Junktown.

In daylight the street was even worse than it had
appeared the night before. For the most part the
rows of old town houses and Victorian mansions
were neglected and forlorn. Some had been made
into rooming houses, while others were disfigured
with added storefronts. The gutters were choked
with an alloy of trash and gray ice, and refuse cans
stood frozen to the unshoveled sidewalks.

"This neighborhood's an eyesore," the cab driver
remarked. "The city should tear it down."

"Don't worry. They will!" Qwilleran said with
optimism.

As soon as he spotted antique shops, he stopped
the cab and got out without enthusiasm. He surveyed the gloomy street. So this was Christmas in
Junktown! Unlike other shopping areas in the city,
Zwinger Street was devoid of holiday decorations.
No festoons spanned the wide thoroughfare; no glit-
tering angels trumpeted from the light poles. Pedestrians were few, and cars barreled past with whining
snow tires, in a hurry to be elsewhere.

A wintry blast from the northeast sent Qwilleran
hurrying toward the first store that professed to sell
antiques. It was dark within, and the door was
locked, but he cupped his hands to his temples and

looked through the glass. What he saw was a gigantic wood carving of a gnarled tree with five lifesize monkeys swinging from its branches. One monkey held a hatrack. One monkey held a lamp. One monkey held a mirror. One monkey held a clock. One monkey held an umbrella stand.

Qwilleran backed away.

Nearby was the shop called The Three Weird Sisters. The store was closed, although a card in the window insisted it was open.

The newsman turned up his coat collar and covered his ears with gloved hands, wishing he had not had his hair trimmed. He next tried the Junque Trunque—closed—and a basement shop called Tech-Tiques, which looked as if it had never been open. Between the antique shops there were commercial establishments with dirty windows, and in one of these—a hole in the wall labeled Popopopoulos' Fruit, Cigars, Work Gloves and Sundries—he bought a pouch of tobacco and found it to be stale.

With growing disaffection for his assignment he walked past a dilapidated barbershop and a third-class nursing home until he reached a large antique shop on the corner. Its door was padlocked, and its windows were plastered with notices of an auction. Qwilleran, looking through the glass door, saw dusty furniture, clocks, mirrors, a bugle made into a lamp, and marble statues of Greek maidens in coy poses.

He also saw the reflection of another man approaching the store. The figure came up behind him with a faltering step, and a thick voice said amiably, "You like 'at slop?"

Qwilleran turned and faced an early-morning drunk, red-eyed and drooling but amiable. He was wearing a coat obviously made from a well-used horse blanket.

"Know what it is? Slop!" the man repeated with a moist grin as he peered through the door at the antiques. Relishing the wetness of the word, he turned to Qwilleran and said it again with embellishments. "Ssssloppp!"

The newsman moved away in disgust and wiped his face with a handkerchief, but the intruder was determined to be friendly.

"You can't get in," he explained helpfully. "Door locked. Locked it after the murder." Perhaps he caught a flicker of interest in Qwilleran's face, because he added, "Stabbed! Sssstabbed!" It was another juicy word, and he illustrated it by plunging an imaginary dagger into the newsman's stomach.

"Get lost!" Qwilleran muttered and strode away.

Nearby there was a carriage house converted into a refinishing shop. Qwilleran tried that door, too, knowing it would not open, and he was right.

He was beginning to have an uneasy feeling about this street, as if the antique shops were fakes—stage props. Where were the proprietors? Where were the collectors who paid twenty-eight dollars for an old tin box? The only people in sight were two children in shabby snowsuits, a workman with a lunchpail, an old lady in black, who was plodding along with a shopping bag, and the good-natured drunk, now sitting on the frozen sidewalk.

At that moment Qwilleran looked up and saw movement in a curved bay window—a clean, sparkling window in a narrow town house painted dark gray with fresh black trim and a fine brass knocker on the door. The building had a residential look, but there was a discreet sign: The Blue Dragon—Antiques.

Slowly he mounted the flight of eight stone steps and tried the door, fearing it would be locked, but to his surprise it opened, and he stepped into an entrance hall of great elegance and formality. There was an Oriental rug on the waxed floor and delicate Chinese paper on the walls. A gilded mirror crowned with three carved plumes hung over a well-polished table that held chrysanthemums in a porcelain bowl. There was a fragrance of exotic wood. There was also the hush of death, except for the ticking of a clock.

Qwilleran, standing there in amazement, suddenly felt he was being watched, and he turned on his heel, but it was only a blackamoor, a lifesize ebony carving of a Nubian slave with turbaned head and an evil glint in his jeweled eyes.

Now the newsman was convinced that Junktown was something less than real. This was the enchanted palace in the depths of the dark forest.

A blue velvet rope barred the stairway, but the parlor doors stood open invitingly, and Qwilleran advanced with caution into a high-ceilinged room filled with furniture, paintings, silver, and blue and white china. A silver chandelier hung from the sculptured plaster ceiling.

His footsteps made the floor creak, and he coughed self-consciously. Then he caught a glimpse of something blue in the window—a large blue porcelain dragon—and he was moving toward it when he almost fell over a foot. It looked like a human foot in an embroidered slipper. He sucked in his breath sharply and stepped back. A lifesize female figure in a long blue satin kimono was seated in a carved Oriental chair. One elbow rested on the arm of the chair, and the slender hand held a cigarette holder. The face seemed to be made of porcelain—blue-white porcelain—and the wig was blue-black.

Qwilleran started to breathe again, thankful he had not knocked the thing over, and then he noticed smoke curling from the tip of the cigarette. It—or she—was alive.

"Are you looking for anything in particular?" she asked coolly. Only the lips moved in her masklike face. Her large dark eyes, heavily rimmed with black pencil, fixed themselves on the newsman without expression.

"No. Just looking," said Qwilleran with a gulp.

"There are two more rooms in the rear, and eighteenth century oils and engravings in the basement." She spoke with a cultivated accent.

The newsman studied her face, making mental notes for the story he would write: wide cheekbones, hollow cheeks, flawless complexion, blue-black hair worn Oriental style, haunting eyes, earrings of jade. She was about thirty, he guessed—an age to which he was partial. He relaxed.

"I'm from the *Daily Fluxion*," he said in his most agreeable voice, "and I'm about to write a series on Junktown."

"I prefer to have no publicity," she said with a frozen stare.

Only three times in his twenty-five years of newspapering had he heard anyone decline to be mentioned in print, and all three had been fugitives—from the law, from blackmail, from a nagging wife. But here was something incomprehensible: the operator of a business enterprise refusing publicity. *Free* publicity.

"All the other shops seem to be closed," he said.

"They should open at eleven, but antique dealers are seldom punctual."

Qwilleran looked around aimlessly and said, "How much for the blue dragon in the window?"

"It's not for sale." She moved the cigarette holder to her lips and drew on it exquisitely. "Are you interested in Oriental porcelains? I have a blue and white stemmed cup from the Hsuan Te period."

"No, I'm just digging for stories. Know anything about the auction sale down at the corner?"

She coughed on the cigarette smoke, and for the first time her poise wavered. "It's at one thirty today," she said.

"I know. I saw the sign. Who was this dealer who was killed?"

Her voice dropped to a lower pitch. "Andrew Glanz. A highly respected authority on antiques."

"When did it happen?"

"The sixteenth of October."

"Was it a holdup? I don't remember reading about a murder in Junktown, and I usually follow the crime news carefully."

"What makes you think it was—murder?" she said with a wary glint in her unblinking eyes.

"I heard someone say—and in this kind of neighborhood, you know . . ."

"He was killed in an accident."

"Traffic accident?"

"He fell from a ladder." She crushed her cigarette. "I would rather not talk about it. It was too—too—"

"He was a friend of yours?" Qwilleran asked in the sympathetic tone that had won him the confidence of maidens and murderers in the past.

"Yes. But, if you don't mind, Mr.—Mr.—"

"Qwilleran."

"The name is Irish?" She was deliberately changing the subject.

"No, Scottish. Spelled with a Qw. And your name?"

"Duckworth."

"Miss or Mrs.?"

She drew a breath. "Miss. . . . I have quite a few

antiques from Scotland in the other room. Would you like to see them?"

She rose and led the way. She was tall and slender, and the kimono, a long shaft of blue, moved with silky grace among the mahogany sideboards and walnut tables.

"These andirons are Scottish," she said, "and so is this brass salver. Do you like brass? Most men like brass."

Qwilleran was squinting at something leaning against the wall in a far corner. "What's that?" he demanded. He pointed to a wrought-iron coat of arms, a yard in diameter. It was a shield surrounded by three snarling cats.

"An ornament from an iron gate, I think. It may have come from the arch over the gate of a castle."

"It's the Mackintosh coat of arms!" said Qwilleran. "I know the inscription: *Touch not the catt bot a glove*. My mother was a Mackintosh." He patted his moustache with satisfaction.

"You ought to buy it," Miss Duckworth said.

"What would I do with it? I don't even have an apartment. How much is it?"

"I've been asking two hundred dollars, but if you like it, you can have it for one hundred twenty-five dollars. That's actually what I paid for it." She lifted the weighty piece out from the wall to show it off to better advantage. "You'll never find a better buy, and you can always sell it for what you paid—or more. That's the nice thing about antiques. It would be wonderful over a fireplace—against a chimney wall. See, it has remnants of a lovely old red and blue decoration."

As she warmed to her sales talk, she grew animated and her dark-rimmed eyes glistened. Qwilleran began to feel mellow. He began to regard this blue-white porcelain creature as a possible prospect for Christmas Eve at the Press Club.

"I'll think about it," he said, turning away from the coat of arms with reluctance. "Meanwhile, I'm going to cover the auction this afternoon. Do you happen to know where I could get a picture of Andrew Glanz to use with my story?"

Her reserved manner returned. "What—what kind of story are you going to write?"

"I'll just describe the auction and give suitable recognition to the deceased."

She hesitated, glancing at the ceiling.

"If it's true what you say, Miss Duckworth—that he was a highly respected authority—"

"I have a few pictures in my apartment upstairs. Would you like to look at them?"

She unhooked the velvet rope that barred the stairs. "Let me go first and restrain the dog."

At the top of the stairs a large German police dog was waiting with unfriendly growl and quivering jaws. Miss Duckworth penned him in another room and then led the newsman down a long hallway, its walls covered with framed photographs. Qwilleran thought he recognized some rather important people in those frames. Of the deceased dealer there were three pictures: Glanz on a lecture platform, Glanz with the director of the historical museum, and then a studio portrait—a photograph of a young man with a square jaw, firm mouth, and intelligent eyes—a good face, an honest face.

Qwilleran glanced at Miss Duckworth, who was clasping and unclasping her hands, and said, "May I borrow this studio shot? I'll have it copied and return it."

She nodded sadly.

"You have a beautiful apartment," he said, glancing into a living room that was all gold velvet, blue silk, and polished wood. "I had no idea there was anything like this in Junktown."

"I wish other responsible people would buy some of the old houses and preserve them," she said. "So far the only ones who have shown any inclination to do so are the Cobbs. They have the mansion on this block. Antiques on the first floor and apartments upstairs."

"Apartments? Do you know if they have one for rent?"

"Yes," the girl said, lowering her eyes. "There's one vacant in the rear."

"I might inquire about it. I need a place to live."

"Mrs. Cobb is a very pleasant woman. Don't let her husband upset you."

"I don't upset easily. What's wrong with her husband?"

Miss Duckworth turned her attention to the downstairs hall. Customers had walked into the house and were chattering and exclaiming. "You go down," she instructed Qwilleran, "and I'll let the dog out of the kitchen before I follow you."

Downstairs two women were wandering among the treasures—women with the air and facial characteristics of suburban housewives; the newsman had met hundreds of them at flower shows and amateur art exhibits. But the garb of these women was out of character. One wore a man's leather trench coat and a woolly mop of a hat studded with seashells, while the other was bundled up in an Eskimo parka over black-and-white checkerboard trousers stuffed into hunting boots with plaid laces.

"Oh, what a lovely shop," said the parka.

"Oh, she's got some old Steuben," said the trench coat.

"Oh, Freda, look at this decanter! My grandmother had one just like it. Wonder what she wants for it."

"She's high, but she has good things. Don't act too enthusiastic, and she'll come down a few dollars," the trench coat advised, adding in a low voice, "Did you know she was Andy's girl friend?"

"You mean—Andy, the one who . . . ?"

The trench coat nodded. "You know how he was killed, don't you?"

The other one shuddered and made a grimace of distaste.

"Here she comes."

As Miss Duckworth glided into the room, looking cool, poised, fragile as bone china—Qwilleran went to the rear of the shop to have one more look at the

Mackintosh coat of arms. It was massive and crudely made. He felt a need to touch it, and his flesh tingled as his hand made contact with the iron. Then he hefted it—with an involuntary grunt. It felt like a hundred-pound weight.

And yet, he remembered afterwards, the delicate Miss Duckworth had lifted it with apparent ease.

THREE

By noon Zwinger Street showed signs of coming to life. A halfhearted winter sunshine had broken through the gloom, adding no real joy to the scene— only a sickly smile. The sidewalks were now populated with women and quite a few men in their antiquing clothes—deliberately outlandish, mismatched, or shabby. They moved from shop to shop while waiting for the auction at one thirty.

Qwilleran decided there was time for a quick lunch and found a diner, where he gulped a leathery hot dog on a spongy roll, a beverage claiming to be coffee and a piece of synthetic pie with crust made of papier-mâché. He also telephoned the feature editor and asked for a photographer.

"About this auction," he told Arch Riker. "We should get some candids of the crowd. Their getups are incredible."

"I told you Junktown was colorful," Riker reminded him.

"Don't send me Tiny Spooner. He's a clumsy oaf, and there are lots of breakables here."

"At this short notice we'll have to take any man we can get. Have you bought any antiques yet?"

"NO!" Qwilleran bellowed into the mouthpiece, at the same time thinking warmly of the Mackintosh coat of arms.

By one o'clock the scene of the auction was crowded. Andrew Glanz had done business in a large building, probably dating from the 1920s when the neighborhood had begun to go commercial. The high ceiling was hung with ladderback chair, copper pots, birdcages, sleds, and chandeliers of every description. The floor was crowded with furniture in a disorganized jumble, pushed back to make room for rows of folding chairs. A narrow stairway led to a balcony, and from its railings hung Oriental rugs and faded tapestries. Everywhere there were signs reminding customers, "If you break it, you've bought it."

The auctiongoers were circulating, examining the merchandise with studious frowns, looking at the underside of plates, ringing crystal with a flick of a finger.

Qwilleran pushed through the crowd, making mental notes of the conversation around him.

"Look at this rocking horse! I had one exactly like it in the attic, and my husband burned it in the fireplace!"

"If it has a little man with a parasol on the bridge, it's Canton china, but if he's sitting in the teahouse, it's Nanking . . . or maybe it's the other way around."

"What's this thing? It would make a wonderful punch bowl!"

"I don't see the finial anywhere, thank God!"

"There's Andy's stepladder."

"My grandmother had a Meissen ewer, but hers was blue."

"Do you think they'll put up the finial?"

As the auction hour approached, people began to take seats facing the platform, and Qwilleran found a chair at the end of a row where he could watch for the *Fluxion* photographer to arrive. There were all kinds, all ages in the audience. One man in a Hudson Bay blanket coat carried a small dog dressed to match. Another was wearing a Santa Claus cap and a rainbow-striped muffler that hung down to the floor.

Next to Qwilleran sat a plump woman with two pairs of glasses hanging from ribbons around her neck.

"This is my first auction," he said to her. "Do you have any advice for a greenhorn?"

The woman had been designed with a compass:

large round pupils in round eyes in a round face. She gave him a half-circular smile. "Don't scratch your ear, or you'll find you've bought that pier mirror." She pointed to a narrow mirror in an ornate frame that towered a good fourteen feet high and leaned against the balcony rail. "I was afraid I'd miss the auction. I had to go to the eye doctor, and he kept me waiting. He put drops in my eyes, and I can't see a thing."

"What's the finial that everyone's talking about?"

She shivered. "Don't you know about Andy's accident?"

"I heard he fell off a ladder."

"Worse than that!" She made a pained face. "Let's skip the details. It makes me sick to my stomach. . . . At first I thought you were an out-of-town dealer."

"I'm from the *Daily Fluxion*."

"Really?" She smoothed her ash-colored hair and turned adoring pupils in his direction. "Are you going to write up the auction? I'm Iris Cobb. My husband runs The Junkery down the street."

"You must be the people with the apartment to rent."

"Are you interested? You'd love it! It's furnished with antiques." The woman kept glancing toward the door. "Wonder if my husband is here yet. I can't see a thing."

"What does he look like?"

"Tall and nice-looking and probably needs a shave. He'll be wearing a red flannel shirt."

"He's standing at the back, next to a grandfather's clock."

The woman settled back in her chair. "I'm glad he got here. He'll do the bidding, and I won't have to worry about it."

"He's talking to a character in a Santa Claus cap."

"That must be Ben Nicholas. Ben rents one of our apartments and runs a shop called Bit o' Junk." With an affectionate smile she added, "He's an idiot!"

"Anyone else I should know? There's a blond guy on crutches, all dressed in white."

"Russell Patch, the refinisher. He never wears anything but white." She lowered her voice. "In front of us—the thin man—he's Hollis Prantz. He has a new shop called Tech-Tiques. The man with the briefcase is Robert Maus, attorney for the estate."

Qwilleran was impressed. The firm of Teahandle, Burris, Hansblow, Maus and Castle was the most prestigious in the city.

"Mr. Maus has a personal interest in Junktown," Mrs. Cobb explained. "Otherwise—"

The rapping of a gavel interrupted the conversation in the audience, and the auctioneer opened the sale. He wore a dark business suit with a plaid shirt, string tie, and Texas boots.

"We have a lot of good goods here today," he said, "and some smart cookies in the audience, so bid fast if you want to buy. Please refrain from unnecessary yakking so I can hear spoken bids. Let's go!" He struck the lectern with an ivory hammer. "We'll start with a Bennington houndhandle pitcher—collector's dream—slight chip but what's the difference? Who'll give me five? Five is bid—now six? Six is bid—do I hear seven? Seven over here. Eight over there—anybody give nine?—eight I've got—sold for eight!"

There were protests from the audience.

"Too fast for you clods, eh? If you want to buy, keep on your toes," the auctioneer said crisply. "We've got a lot of stuff to move this afternoon."

"He's good," Mrs. Cobb whispered to Qwilleran. "Wait till he really gets wound up!"

Every sixty seconds another item went down under the hammer—a silver inkwell, pewter goblets, a pair of bisque figures, a prayer rug, an ivory snuffbox. Three assistants were kept busy up and down the aisles, while porters carried items to and from the platform.

"And now we have a fine, fat, cast-iron stove," said the auctioneer, raising his voice. "We won't lug it to the platform, because you eagle eyes can see it on the stair landing. Who'll give me fifty?"

All heads turned to look at a sculptured black monster with a bloated silhouette and bowlegged stance.

"Fifty I have—who'll say seventy-five?—it's a beauty. . . . Seventy-five is bid—do I hear a hundred?—you're getting it cheap. . . . I have a hundred—what do I hear? . . . Hundred and ten—it's worth twice the price. . . . Hundred-twenty is bid. . . . Hundred-thirty back there—don't lose this prize—a nice big stove—big enough to hide a body. . . . Hundred-forty is bid—make it a hundred-fifty. . . . *Sold* for a hundred-fifty." The auctioneer turned to the assistant who recorded sales. "Sold to C.C. Cobb."

Mrs. Cobb gasped. "That fool!" she said. "We'll never get our money out of it! I'll bet Ben Nicholas was bidding against him. The bids were going up too fast. Ben didn't want that stove. He was bidding just to be funny. He does it all the time. He knew C.C. wouldn't let him have it." She turned around and glared with unseeing eyes in the direction of the red flannel shirt and the Santa Claus cap.

The auctioneer was saying, "And now before we take an intermission, we'll unload a few items of office equipment."

There were reference books, a filing cabinet, a portable tape recorder, a typewriter—mundane items that had little interest for the crowd of junkers. Mrs. Cobb made a hesitant bid on the tape recorder and got it for a pittance.

"And here we have a portable typewriter—sold as is—one letter missing—who'll give me fifty?—do I hear fifty?—I'll take forty—I think it's the Z that's missing—I'm waiting for forty—thirty, then—who'll say thirty?"

"Twenty," said Qwilleran, to his own surprise.

"Sold to the astute gentleman with the big mous-

tache for twenty smackers and now we'll take a fif-
teen-minute break."

Qwilleran was stunned by his windfall. He had
not expected to do any bidding.

"Let's stretch our legs," Mrs. Cobb said, pulling
at his sleeve in a familiar way.

As they stood up they were confronted by the
man in the red flannel shirt. "Why'd you buy that
stupid tape recorder?" he demanded of his wife.

"You wait and see!" she said with a saucy shake
of her head. "This is a reporter from the *Daily Fluxion*. He's interested in our vacant apartment."

"It's not for rent. I don't like reporters," Cobb
growled and walked away with his hands in his
trouser pockets.

"My husband is the most obnoxious dealer in
Junktown," Mrs. Cobb said with pride. "Don't you
think he's good-looking?"

Qwilleran was trying to think of a tactful reply
when there was a crash near the front door, followed by exclamations and groans. The *Fluxion*
photographer was standing at the entrance.

Tiny Spooner was six-feet-three and weighed close
to four hundred pounds, including the photographic
equipment draped about his person. Added to his
obesity were cameras, lens cases, meters, lights, film
kits, and folding tripods dangling from straps and
connected by trailing cords.

Mrs. Cobb said, "What a shame! Must have been
the Sèvres vase on the Empire pedestal."

"Was it valuable?"

"Worth about eight hundred dollars, I guess."

"Save my seat for me," Qwilleran said. "I'll be right back."

Tiny Spooner was standing near the door, looking uncomfortable. "So help me, I'm innocent," he told Qwilleran. "I was nowhere near the silly thing." He shifted the equipment that hung around his neck and over both shoulders, and his tripod whacked a bust of Marie Antoinette. Qwilleran flung his arms around the white marble.

"Oops," said Tiny.

The auctioneer was looking at the remains of the Sèvres vase, instructing the porter to gather the shattered fragments carefully, and Qwilleran thought it was time to introduce himself.

"We want to get a few candid shots during the bidding," he told the auctioneer. "You can proceed normally. Don't pay any attention to the photographer."

Spooner said, "I'd like to get some elevation and shoot down. Do you have a stepladder?"

There was an awkward pause. Someone laughed nervously.

"Skip it," said the photographer. "I see there's a balcony. I'll shoot from the stairway."

"Take it easy," Qwilleran cautioned him. "If you break it, you've bought it."

Spooner surveyed the scene with scorn. "Do you want form or content? I don't know what I can do with this rubbish. Too many dynamic lines and no chiaroscuro." He waddled toward the stairway, his photo equipment swinging, and the wagging tripod narrowly missed the crown glass doors of a breakfront.

Back in his seat, Qwilleran explained to Mrs. Cobb, "He's the only press photographer I know with a Ph.D. in mathematics, but he's inclined to be clumsy."

"My goodness!" she said. "If he's so smart, why is he working for a newspaper?"

The gavel rapped, and the second half of the auction began, bringing out the most desirable items: an English bookcase, a Boule commode, a seventeenth century Greek icon, a small collection of Benin bronzes.

Occasionally there was a flash from the photographer's lights, and women in the audience touched their hair and assumed bright, intelligent expressions.

"And now," said the auctioneer, "we have this beautiful pair of French chairs in the original—"

There was a shriek!

A shout: "Look out!"

A porter lunged forward with arms outstretched, barely in time to steady a teetering mirror—the pier mirror that almost reached the ceiling. In another second the towering glass would have crashed on the audience.

The spectators gasped, and Qwilleran said, "Whew!" At the same time he scanned the crowd for Spooner.

The photographer was leaning over the balcony railing. He caught the newsman's eye and shrugged.

Mrs. Cobb said, "I've never seen so many accidents at an auction! It gives me the creeps. Do you believe in ghosts?"

The audience was nervous and noisy. The auctioneer raised his voice and increased the tempo of his spiel. Waving his hand, jabbing his finger at bidders, jerking his thumb over his shoulder when each item was sold, he whipped the spectators into a frenzy.

"Do you want this or don't you?—Five hundred I've got—Do I hear six hundred?—What's the matter with you?—it's two hundred years old!—I want seven—I want seven—I'll buy it myself for seven—going, going—take it away!" The thumb jerked, the gavel crashed on the lectern, and the excitement in the audience reached a crescendo.

The two-hundred-year-old desk was removed, and the spectators waited eagerly for the next item.

At this point there was a significant pause in the action, as the auctioneer spoke to the attorney. It was a pantomime of indecision. Then they both nodded and beckoned to a porter. A moment later a hush fell on the crowd. The porter had placed a curious object on the platform—a tall, slender ornament about three feet high. It had a square base topped by a brass ball, and then a shaft of black metal tapering up to a swordlike point.

"That's it!" someone whispered behind Qwilleran. "That's the finial!"

Beside him, Mrs. Cobb was shaking her head and covering her face with her hands. "They shouldn't have done it!"

"We have here," said the auctioneer in slow, deliberate tones, "the finial from a rooftop—probably an ornament from an old house in the Zwinger reclamation area. The ball is solid brass. Needs a little polishing. What am I offered?"

The people seated around Qwilleran were shocked.

"Makes my blood run cold," one whispered.

"I didn't think they'd have the nerve to put it up."

"Who's bidding? Can you see who's bidding?"

"Very bad taste! Very bad!" someone said.

"Did Andy actually fall on it?"

"Didn't you know? He was impaled!"

"Sold!" snapped the auctioneer. "Sold to C.C. Cobb."

"No!" cried Mrs. Cobb.

At that moment there was a spine-chilling crash. A bronze chandelier let loose from the ceiling and crashed on the floor, narrowly missing Mr. Maus, the attorney.

FOUR

It had been a splendid Victorian mansion in its day—a stately red brick with white columns framing the entrance, a flight of broad steps, and a railing of ornamental ironwork. Now the painted trim was peeling, and the steps were cracked and crumbling.

This was the building that housed the Cobbs' antique shop, The Junkery, and the bay windows on either side of the entrance were filled with colored glass and bric-a-brac.

After the auction Qwilleran accompanied Mrs. Cobb to the mansion, and she left him in the tacky entrance hall.

"Have a look at our shop," she said, "while I go upstairs and see if the apartment is presentable. We've been selling out of it for two months, and it's probably a mess."

"It's been vacant two months?" Qwilleran asked, counting back to October. "Who was your last tenant?"

Mrs. Cobb looked apologetic. "Andy Glanz lived up there. You don't mind, do you? Some people are squeamish."

She hurried upstairs, and Qwilleran inspected the hallway. Although shabby, it was graciously wide, with carved woodwork and elaborate gaslight fixtures converted for electricity. The rooms opening off the hall were filled with miscellany in various stages of decrepitude. One room was crowded with fragments of old buildings—porch posts, fireplaces, slabs of discolored marble, stained-glass windows, an iron gate and sections of stair railing. Customers who had drifted in after the auction were poking among the debris, appraising with narrowed eyes, exhibiting a lack of enthusiasm. They were veteran junkers.

Eventually Qwilleran found himself in a room filled with cradles, brass beds, trunks, churns, weather vanes, flatirons, old books, engravings of Abraham Lincoln, and a primitive block and tackle made into a lamp. There was also a mahogany bar with brass rail, evidently salvaged from a turn-of-the-century saloon, and behind it stood a red-shirted man, unshaven and handsome in a brutal way. He watched Qwilleran with a hostile glare.

The newsman ignored him and picked up a book from one of the tables. It was bound in leather, and the cracking spine was lettered in gold that had worn away with age. He opened the book to find the title page.

"*Don't* open that book," came a surly command, "unless you're buying it."

Qwilleran's moustache bristled. "How do I know whether I want it till I read the title?"

"To hell with the title!" said the proprietor. "If you like the looks of it, buy it. If you don't, keep your sweatin' hands in your pockets. How long do you think those books will last if every jerk that comes in here has to paw the bindings?"

"How much do you want for it?" Qwilleran demanded.

"I don't think I want to sell it. Not to you, anyway."

The other customers had stopped browsing and were looking mildly amused at Qwilleran's discomfiture. He sensed the encouragement in their glances and rose to the occasion.

"Discrimination! That's what this is," he roared. "I should report this and have you put out of business! This place is a rat's nest anyway. The city should condemn it. . . . Now, how much do you want for this crummy piece of junk?"

"Four bucks, just to shut your loud mouth!"

"I'll give you three." Qwilleran threw some bills on the bar.

Cobb scooped them up and filed them in his billfold. "Well, there's more than one way to skin a sucker," he said with a leer at the other customers.

Qwilleran opened the book he had bought. It was *The Works of the Reverend Dr. Ishmael Higginbotham, Being a Collection of Interesting Tracts Explaining Several Important Points of the Divine Doctrine, Set Forth with Diligence and Extreme Brevity*.

Mrs. Cobb burst into the room. "Did you let that dirty old man bully you into buying something?"

"Shut up, old lady," said her husband.

She had put on a pink dress, fixed her hair, and applied make-up, and she looked plumply pretty. "Come upstairs with me," she said sweetly, putting a friendly hand on Qwilleran's arm. "We'll have a cozy cup of coffee and let Cornball Cobb fume with jealousy."

Mrs. Cobb started up the creaking staircase, her round hips bobbling from side to side and the backs of her fat knees bulging in a horizontal grin. Qwilleran was neither titillated nor repelled by the sight, but rather saddened that every woman was not blessed with a perfect figure.

"Don't pay any attention to C.C.," she said over her shoulder. "He's a great kidder."

The spacious upstairs hall was a forest of old chairs, tables, desks, and chests. Several doors stood open, revealing dingy living quarters.

"Our apartment is on that side," said Mrs. Cobb, indicating an open door through which came a loud radio commercial, "and on this side we have two smaller apartments. Ben Nicholas rents the front, but the rear is nicer because it has a view of the backyard."

Qwilleran looked out the hall window and saw two station wagons backed in from the alley, an iron bed, a grindstone, the fender from a car, some wagon wheels, an old refrigerator with no door, and a wooden washing machine with attached clothes wringer—most of them frozen together in a drift of dirty ice and snow.

"Then how come Nicholas lives in the front?" he asked.

"His apartment has a bay window, and he can keep an eye on the entrance to his shop, next door."

She led the way into the rear apartment—a large square room with four tall windows and a frightening collection of furniture. Qwilleran's gaze went first to an old parlor organ in jaundiced oak—then a pair of high-backed gilded chairs with seats supported by gargoyles—then a round table, not quite level, draped with an embroidered shawl and holding an oil lamp, its two globes painted with pink roses—then a patterned rug suffering from age and melancholy—then a crude rocking chair made of bent twigs and treebark, probably full of termites.

"You *do* like antiques, don't you?" Mrs. Cobb asked anxiously.

"Not especially," Qwilleran replied in a burst of honesty. "And what is that supposed to be?" He pointed to a chair with tortured iron frame, elevated on a pedestal and equipped with headrest and footrest.

"An old dentist's chair—really quite comfortable for reading. You can pump it up and down with your foot. And the painting over the fireplace is a very good primitive."

With a remarkably controlled expression on his face, Qwilleran studied the lifesize portrait of someone's great-great-grandmother, dressed in black—square-jawed, thin-lipped, steely-eyed, and disapproving all she surveyed.

"You haven't said a word about the daybed," said Mrs. Cobb with enthusiasm. "It's really unique. It came from New Jersey."

The newsman turned around and winced. The daybed, placed against one wall, was built like a swan boat, with one end carved in the shape of a long-necked bad-tempered bird and the other end culminating in a tail.

"Sybaritic," he said drily, and the landlady went into spasms of laughter.

A second room, toward the front of the house, had been subdivided into kitchenette, dressing room, and bath.

Mrs. Cobb said, "C.C. installed the kitchen himself. He's handy with tools. Do you like to cook?"

"No, I take most of my meals at the Press Club."

"The fireplace works, if you want to haul wood upstairs. Do you like the place? I usually get one hundred and ten dollars a month, but if you like it, you can have it for eighty-five dollars."

Qwilleran looked at the furniture again and groomed his moustache thoughtfully. The furnishings gave him a chill, but the rent suited his economic position admirably. "I'd need a desk and a good reading light and a place to put my books."

"We've got anything you want. Just ask for it."

He bounced on the daybed and found it sufficiently firm. Being built down to the floor, it would offer no temptations to burrowing cats. "I forgot to tell you," he said. "I have pets. A couple of Siamese cats."

"Fine! They'll get rid of our mice. They can have a feast."

"I don't think they like meat on the hoof. They prefer it well-aged and served medium rare with pan juices."

Mrs. Cobb laughed heartily—too heartily—at his humor. "What do you call your cats?"

"Koko and Yum Yum."

"Oh, excuse me a minute!" She rushed from the room and returned to explain that she had a pie in the oven. An aroma of apples and spices was wafting across the hall, and Qwilleran's moustache twitched.

While Mrs. Cobb straightened pictures and tested surfaces for dust, Qwilleran examined the facilities. The bathroom had an archaic tub with clawed feet, snarling faucets, and a maze of exposed pipes. The refrigerator was new, however, and the large dressing room had a feature that interested him; one wall was a solid bank of built-in bookshelves filled with volumes in old leather bindings.

"If you want to use the shelves for something else,

we'll move the books out," Mrs. Cobb said. "We found them in the attic. They belonged to the man who built this house over a hundred years ago. He was a newspaper editor. Very prominent in the abolitionist movement. This house is quite historic."

Qwilleran noticed Dostoyevski, Chesterfield, Emerson. "You don't need to move the books, Mrs. Cobb. I might like to browse through them."

"Then you'll take the apartment?" Her round eyes were shining. "Have a cup of coffee and a piece of pie, and then you can decide."

Soon Qwilleran was sitting in a gilded chair at the lopsided table, plunging a fork into bubbling hot pie with sharp cheese melted over the top. Mrs. Cobb watched with pleasure as her prospective tenant devoured every crumb of flaky crust and every dribble of spiced juice.

"Have some more?"

"I shouldn't." Qwilleran pulled in his waistline. "But it's very good."

"Oh, come on! You don't have to worry about weight. You have a very nice physique."

The newsman tackled his second wedge of pie, and Mrs. Cobb described the joys of living in an old house.

"We have a ghost," she announced cheerfully. "A blind woman who used to live here fell down the stairs and was killed. C.C. says her ghost is fascinated by my glasses. When I go to bed, I put them on the night table, and in the morning they're on the window sill. Or if I put them in the dresser drawer, they're moved to the night table. . . . More coffee?"

"Thanks. Do the glasses move around every night?"

"Only when the moon is full." The landlady grew thoughtful. "Do you realize how many strange things happened at the auction today? The Sèvres vase, and the chandelier that fell, and the pier mirror that started to topple. . . . It makes me wonder."

"Wonder what?"

"It's almost as if Andy's spirit was *protesting*."

"Do you believe in that kind of thing?"

"I don't know. I do and I don't."

"What do you think Andy might have been trying to say?" Qwilleran wore a sincere expression. He had a talent for sincerity that had drawn confidences from the most reticent persons.

Mrs. Cobb chuckled. "Probably that the auctioneer was letting things go too cheap. There were some terrific buys."

"All the junkers call Andy's death an accident, but I met someone on the street who said he was murdered."

"No, it was an accident. The police said so. And yet . . ." Her voice trailed away.

"What were you going to say?"

"Well . . . it seems strange that Andy would be careless enough to slip and fall on that thing. He was a very . . . a very *prudent* young man, you know."

Qwilleran smoothed his moustache hurriedly. "I'd like to hear more about Andy," he said. "Why don't I go and get my luggage and the cats . . . ?"

"You'll take the apartment?" Mrs. Cobb clapped

her hands. "I'm so glad! It will be nice to have a professional writer in the house. It will give us *class*, if you know what I mean."

She gave him a key to the downstairs door and accepted a month's rent.

"We don't bother to lock our doors up here," she said, "but if you want a key, I'll find you one."

"Don't worry about it. Nothing that I own is worth locking up."

She gave him a mischievous look. "Mathilda walks right through doors, anyway."

"Who?"

"Mathilda. Our ghost."

Qwilleran went back to his hotel and made one telephone call before packing his suitcases. He called the Photo Lab at the *Daily Fluxion* and asked for Tiny Spooner.

"How'd the pictures turn out, Tiny?"

"Fair. They're on the dryer. Can't say they're graphically articulate. Too many incongruous shapes."

"Leave them in the Feature slot, and I'll pick them up Monday. And Tiny," Qwilleran said, "I want to ask you one question. Give me the truth. Did you or didn't you—"

"I was nowhere near that blasted crockery. I swear! I looked at it, that's all, and it started to jiggle."

"And how about the chandelier and the big mirror?"

"Don't try to pin those on me, either! So help me, I was twenty feet away when they let loose!"

FIVE

The cats knew something was afoot. When Qwilleran returned to Medford Manor, both were huddled in wary anticipation.

"Come on, you guys. We're moving out of Medicare Manor," Qwilleran said.

From the closet he brought the soup carton with airholes punched in the side. Koko had been through this routine twice before, and he consented to hop in, but Yum Yum was having none of it.

"Come on, sweetheart."

Yum Yum responded by turning into a lump of lead, her underside fused to the carpet and anchored

by twenty efficient little hooks. Only when
Qwilleran produced a can opener and a small can
with a blue label did she loosen her grip. With a sen-
suous gurgle in her throat, she leaped onto the
dresser.

"All right, sister," the man said as he grabbed her.
"It was a dirty trick, but I had to do it. We'll open
the chicken when we get to Junktown."

When Qwilleran and his two suitcases, four car-
tons of books, and one carton of cats arrived at the
Cobb mansion, he hardly recognized his apartment.
The dentist's chair and parlor organ were gone, and
the pot-bellied stove from the auction was standing
in one corner. Two lamps had been added: a reading
lamp sprouting out of a small brass cash register,
and a floor lamp that had once been a musket. The
elderly battle-ax over the fireplace still glowered at
him, and the depressing rug was still grieving on the
floor, but there were certain improvements: a roll-
top desk, a large open cupboard for books, and an
old-fashioned Morris chair—a big, square contraption with reclining back, soft black leather cushions,
and ottoman to match.

As soon as Qwilleran opened the soup carton,
Yum Yum leaped out, dashed insanely in several directions, and ended on top of the tall cupboard.
Koko emerged slowly, with circumspection. He ex-
plored the apartment systematically and thoroughly,
approved the red-cushioned seats of the two gilt
chairs, circled the pot-bellied stove three times and
discovered no earthly use for it, leaped to the mantel

and sniffed the primitive portrait, afterwards rubbing his jaw on the corner of the frame and tilting the picture askew. Then he arranged himself attractively between two brass candlesticks on the mantelshelf.

"Oh, isn't he lovely!" exclaimed Mrs. Cobb, appearing with a stack of clean towels and a cake of soap. "Is that Koko? Hello, Koko. Do you like it here, Koko?" She looked at him in a near-sighted way, waggling a finger at his nose and speaking in the falsetto voice with which cats are often addressed—an approach that always offended Koko. He sneezed in her face, enveloping her in a gossamer mist.

"The cats will like it here," she said, straightening the picture that Koko had nudged. "They can watch the pigeons in the backyard."

She bustled into the bathroom with the towels, and as soon as she turned her back, Koko scraped his jaw with vengeance on the corner of the picture frame, pitching it into a forty-five-degree list.

Qwilleran cleared his throat. "I see you've made a few changes, Mrs. Cobb."

"Right after you left, a customer wanted that dentist's chair, so we sold it. Hope you don't mind. I've given you the pot-bellied stove to fill up the empty corner. How do you like your roll-top desk?"

"My grandfather—"

"The tavern table will be nice for your typewriter. And what do you usually do about your personal laundry? I'll be glad to put it through the automatic washer for you."

"Oh, no, Mrs. Cobb! That's too much trouble."

"Not at all. And please call me Iris." She drew the draperies across the windows—velvet draperies in streaked and faded gold. "I made these out of an old stage curtain. C.C. got it from a theatre that's being torn down."

"Did you do the wall behind the bed?"

"No. That was Andy's idea." The wall was papered with the yellowed pages of old books, set in quaint typefaces. "Andy was quite a bookworm."

"As soon as I unpack and feed the cats," Qwilleran said, "I'd like to talk to you about Andy."

"Why don't you come across the hall when you're settled? I'll be doing my ironing." And then she added, "C.C. has gone to look at a Jacobean dining room set that someone wants to sell."

Qwilleran emptied his suitcases, lined up his books in the open cupboard, put the cats' blue cushion on top of the refrigerator—their favorite perch—and drew their attention to the new location of the unabridged dictionary which served as their new scratching pad. Then he walked across the hall to the Cobbs' apartment. The first thing he noticed was Mrs. Cobb ironing in the big kitchen, and she invited him to sit on a rush-seated chair (A-522-001) at a battered pine table (D-573-091).

"Do you sell out of your apartment?" he asked.

"Constantly! Last Tuesday we had breakfast at a

round oak table, lunch at a cherry dropleaf, and dinner at that pine trestle table."

"Must be hard work, moving the stuff around, up and down stairs."

"You get used to it. Right now I'm not supposed to lift anything. I wrenched my back a couple of months ago."

"How did you get my apartment rearranged so fast?"

"C.C. got Mike to help him. He's the grocer's son. A nice boy, but he thinks antique dealers are batty. We are, of course," she added with a sly glance at her guest.

"Mrs. Cobb—"

"Please call me Iris. Mind if I call you Jim?"

"People call me Qwill."

"Oh, that's nice. I like that." She smiled at the pajamas she was pressing.

"Iris, I wish you'd tell me more about Andy. It might help me write my story about the auction."

She set the electric iron on its heel and gazed into space. "He was a fine young man! Nice personality, honest, intelligent. He was a writer—like you. I admire writers. You'd never guess it, but I was an English major myself."

"What did Andy write?"

"Mostly articles for antique magazines, but he liked to play around with fiction. Some day I should write a book myself! The people you meet in this business!"

"How much do you know about the accident? When did it happen?"

"One evening in October." Iris coughed. "He'd been having dinner with the Dragon at her apartment—"

"You mean Miss Duckworth?"

"We call her the Dragon. She frightens people with that hoity-toity manner, you know. Well, anyway, Andy had dinner with her and then went to his shop for something, and when he didn't return, she went looking for him. She found him in a pool of *blood!*"

"Did she call the police?"

"No. She came flying over here in hysterics, and C.C. called the police. They decided Andy had fallen off the stepladder while getting a chandelier down from the ceiling. They found the light fixture on the floor smashed. It was all crystal. Five long curving crystal arms and a lot of crystal prisms."

"Is it true that he fell on that sharp finial?"

She nodded. "That's one thing that doesn't make sense. Andy was always so careful! In fact, he was a fussbudget. I don't think he would leave that finial standing around where it would be a hazard. Antique dealers are always spraining their backs or rupturing something, but nothing ever happened to Andy. He was very cautious."

"Maybe he had a couple of drinks with Miss Duckworth and got reckless."

"He didn't drink. She probably had a drink or two, but Andy didn't have any bad habits. He was

kind of straitlaced. I always thought he'd make a
good minister of the gospel if he hadn't gone into
the junk business. He was really dedicated. It's a
calling, you know. It gets to be your whole life."

"Could it have been suicide?"

"Oh, no! Andy wasn't the type."

"You never know what goes on in people's
heads—or what kind of trouble—"

"I couldn't believe it. Not about Andy."

Qwilleran drew his pipe and tobacco pouch from
the pocket of his tweed sports coat. "Mind if I
smoke?"

"Go right ahead. Would you like a can of C.C.'s
beer?"

"No, thanks. I'm on the wagon."

With fascination Iris watched the sucking in of
cheeks and soft oompah-oompah of pipe lighting. "I
wish C.C. smoked a pipe. It smells so good!"

The newsman said, "Do you suppose Andy might
have been killed by a prowler?"

"I don't know."

"Can you think of a motive for murder?"

Iris pressed down on the iron while she thought
about it. "I don't know . . . but I'll tell you something if you'll promise not to tell C.C. He would kid
me about it. . . . It was Andy's horoscope. I just happened to read it in the paper. The *Daily Fluxion* has
the best horoscopes, but we get the *Morning Rampage* because it has more pages, and we need lots of
paper for wrapping china and glass."

"And what did the *Morning Rampage* have to say about Andy?"

"His sign was Aquarius. It said he should beware of trickery." She gave Qwilleran a questioning glance. "I didn't read it till the day after he was killed."

The newsman puffed on his pipe with sober mien. "Not what you would call substantial evidence. . . . Was Andy engaged to the Duckworth girl?"

"Not officially, but there was a lot of running back and forth," Iris said with raised eyebrows.

"She's very attractive," Qwilleran remarked, thinking about the Dragon's eyes. "How did she react after Andy was killed?"

"She was all broken up. My, she was broken up! And that surprised me, because she had always been such a cool cucumber. C.C. said Andy probably got her in a family way before he died, but I don't believe it. Andy was too honorable."

"Maybe Andy was more human than you think."

"Well, he died before Halloween, and this is almost Christmas, and the Dragon's still as skinny as a rake handle. . . . But she's changed. She's very moody and withdrawn."

"What will happen to Andy's estate?"

"I don't know. Mr. Maus is handling it. Andy's parents live upstate somewhere."

"How did the other dealers feel about Andy? Was he well liked?

Iris reflected before she answered. "Everyone *re-*

spected Andy—for his ability—but some people thought he was too much of a goody."

"What do you mean?"

"How shall I explain? . . . In this business you have to grab every advantage you can. You work hard without letup and don't make any money. Some months we can hardly make the payments on this house, because C.C. has tied up his cash in something crazy—like the pot-bellied stove—that we won't be able to sell." She wiped her damp forehead on her sleeve. "So if you see a chance to make a good profit, you grab it. . . . But Andy was always leaning over backwards to be *ethical*, and he condemned people who were trying to make an extra dollar or two. I don't say he was wrong, but he carried it too far. That's the only thing I had against him. . . . Don't say that in the paper. On the whole he was a wonderful person. So considerate in unexpected ways!"

"In what ways?"

"Well, for one thing, he was always so nice to Papa Popopopoulos, the fruit man. The rest of us just ignore the lonely old fellow. . . . And then there was Ann Peabody. When the antique dealers had a neighborhood meeting, Andy always made sure that Ann attended, even if he had to carry her. She's ninety years old and still runs a shop, although she hasn't sold so much as a salt dip in four years." The iron was making light passes over a red and grey striped sport shirt. "One good thing about being in this business—you don't have to iron white shirts."

"Was Andy successful—financially?"

"He made a go of it, I guess. He also sold articles to magazines and taught an evening class in antiques at the Y.W.C.A. In this business everybody has to have some kind of job on the side—or else a rich uncle. C.C. is a professional picket. He was on the picket line this morning in that bitter cold."

"What was he picketing?"

"I don't know. He goes wherever the agency sends him. He likes the work, and it pays time and a half in bad weather."

"Does Miss Duckworth have a sideline?"

"I doubt whether she needs one. I think she has money. She sells very fine things—to a select clientele. She has a Sheraton card table over there that I'd commit murder to own! It's priced way out of my class."

"I was surprised to find such an expensive shop in Junktown."

"I suppose she wanted to be near her boy friend. In this business, location is unimportant; customers will go anywhere to find what they're looking for."

"But isn't there some risk in having valuable things in a neighborhood like this?" Qwilleran asked.

Iris frowned at him. "You're just like everyone else! You think an old neighborhood that's run down is a hotbed of crime. It's not true! We don't have any trouble." She fell silent as she concentrated on the collar of a blouse.

The newsman stood up. "Well, I'd better get back

to work—try out the new typewriter—and see if I can write something about the auction."

"By the way," said Iris, "there's a box of old keys on that Empire chest. See if one of them fits your lock."

He glanced in the box and saw nothing but old-fashioned keys, four inches long. "I don't need to lock my door," he said.

Returning to his apartment, Qwilleran opened the door and reached in for the wall switch that activated three sources of light: the reading light near the Morris chair, the floor lamp standing at the desk, and the hand-painted relic on the tilted table. Then he looked for the cats, as he always did upon coming home.

There they were—sitting on the two gilt chairs like two reigning heads of state on their thrones— with brown paws tucked fastidiously under white breasts and brown ears worn like two little crowns.

"You guys look pretty contented," Qwilleran remarked. "Didn't take you long to feel at home."

Koko squeezed his eyes and said, "Yow," and Yum Yum, whose eyes were slightly crossed, peered at Qwilleran with her perpetual I-don't-know-what-you're-talking-about look and murmured something. Her normal speaking voice was a soprano shriek, but in her softer moments she uttered a high-pitched "Mmmm" with her mouth closed.

The newsman went to work. He opened the typewriter case, hit a few keys on his newly acquired machine and thought, Andy may have been prudent, ethical, intelligent, and good-looking, but he kept a scruffy typewriter. It was filled with eraser crumbs, and the ribbon had been hammered to shreds. Furthermore, the missing letter was not the expendable Z but the ubiquitous E. Qwilleran began to write:

"Th* spirit of th* lat* Andr*w Glanz hov*r*d ov*r Junktown wh*n th* tr*asur*s of this highly r*sp*ct*d d*al*r w*r* sold at auction to th* cr*am of th* city's junk*rs."

He described the cream: their purposely raffish clothes, their wacky conversations, the calculated expressions on their faces. He had made no notes during the day; after twenty-five years of newspapering, his mind was a video tape recorder.

It was slow work, however. The tavern table was rickety. The lack of an E was frustrating, and the asterisks—inserted for the benefit of the typesetter—dazzled his eyes. Between paragraphs, moreover, a pair of piercing eyes kept boring into his consciousness. He knew that kind of stare. It indicated one of two things. The elegant Miss Duckworth was either myopic—or frightened.

At one point Qwilleran was alerted by a low rumble coming from Koko's throat, and soon afterward he heard footsteps slowly mounting the stairs and entering the front apartment. Some minutes later he heard a telephone ring in the adjoining rooms. Then the heavy footsteps started down the hall again.

Qwilleran's curiosity sent him hurrying to the door for a close-up of the man who wore a Santa Claus cap. He saw instead a Napoleonic bicorne perched squarely above a round face that lacked eyebrows.

The man threw up his hands in exaggerated surprise. His small bloodshot eyes stretched wide in astonishment. "Sir! You startled us!" he said in an overly dramatic voice.

"Sorry. Didn't mean to. I just moved in here. My name's Qwilleran."

"Welcome to our humble abode," said the man with a sweeping gesture. He suddenly looked down. "And what have we here?"

Koko had followed Qwilleran into the hall and was rubbing against the stranger's rubber boots in an affectionate way.

"I've never seen him do that before," Qwilleran said. "Koko usually doesn't warm up to strangers right away."

"They know! They know! Ben Nicholas is the friend of bird and beast!"

"You have a shop next door, I understand. I'm with the *Daily Fluxion*, and I'm writing a series on Junktown."

"Pray visit us and write a few kind words. We need the publicity."

"Tomorrow," Qwilleran promised.

"Till then!" With an airy wave of the hand the dealer started downstairs, his ridiculously long scarf dragging on the carpeted treads behind him. "A customer awaits us," he explained. "We must be off."

Mrs. Cobb was right, Qwilleran thought. Ben

Nicholas was an idiot, but Koko evidently approved.

Again all was quiet in the hall beyond Qwilleran's door. Recklessly the newsman wrote about things he did not understand (a M*iss*n armorial sucri*r, *arly Am*rican tr**n, and A Qu*zal compot* in quincunx d*sign), making frequent trips to the dictionary.

After a while, as he sat there pounding out copy with the two long fingers of each hand, he thought he saw—out of the corner of his eye—something moving. He turned his head and looked over his roll-top desk just in time to see the door slowly opening inward. It opened a few inches and stopped.

"Yes? Who is it?" Qwilleran demanded.

There was no answer. He jumped up and went to the door, opening it wide. No one was there, but at the end of the hall, in a jumble of furniture, there was a flicker of movement. Qwilleran pressed his weary eyeballs with his fingers and then stared at the confusion of mahogany, pine, and walnut—legs, lids, drawers, seats, and backs He saw it again—behind a low blanket chest. It was the tip of a brown tail.

"Koko!" he said sharply.

There was no reply from the cat.

"Koko, come back here!" He knew it was Koko; there was no kink in the tail tip.

The cat ignored him, as he customarily did when concentrating on important business of his own.

Qwilleran strode down the hall and saw Koko

disappear behind the parlor organ. The man could guess how the cat had managed to get out. Old houses had loosely fitting doors with weak latches, or else they had swollen doors, thick with paint, that refused to close at all. Koko had pulled the door open with his claws. He was clever about doors; he knew when to pull and when to push.

The man leaned over a marble-topped commode and peered behind the parlor organ. "Get out of there, Koko! It's none of your business."

The cat had leaped to a piano stool. He was sniffing intently. With whiskers back, he moved his nose like a delicate instrument up and down the length of a sharp metal object with a brass ball at its base.

Qwilleran's moustache bristled. The cat had walked out of the apartment and had gone directly to the finial. He was sniffing it with mouth open and fangs bared, a sign of repugnance.

Qwilleran reached behind the organ and grabbed Koko around the middle. The cat squawked as if he were being strangled.

"Mrs. Cobb!" the man called through the open door of his landlady's apartment. "I've changed my mind. I want a key."

While she rummaged through the keybox, he touched his moustache gingerly. There was an odd feeling in the roots of it—a tingling sensation he had experienced several times before. It always happened when there was murder in the air.

SIX

Late that evening Qwilleran sampled the abolitionist's library and became fascinated by a volume of bound copies of *The Liberator*, and it was after midnight when he realized he had nothing in the apartment for breakfast. He had noticed an all-night grocery on the corner, so he put on his overcoat and the latest acquisition in his wardrobe, a porkpie hat in black and white checked tweed with a rakish red feather. It was the reddest red feather he had ever seen, and he liked red.

He locked the door with a four-inch key and went down the squeaking stairs. Snow had begun to fall—

in a kindly way this time, without malice—and Qwilleran stood on the front steps to enjoy the scene. Traffic was sparse, and with the dimness of the outdated streetlights and the quaintness of the buildings and the blessing of the snow, Junktown had an old-time charm. The snow sugared the carved lintels of doors and windows, voluted iron railings, tops of parked cars, and lids of trash cans.

At the nearby intersection there was a glow on the whitened sidewalks, spilling out from the grocery, the drugstore, and the bar called The Lion's Tail. A man came out of the bar, walking with uncertain dignity and clutching for a handrail that did not exist. A girl in tight trousers and spotted fur jacket sauntered past the Cobb mansion, staring at passing cars. Catching sight of Qwilleran, she slithered in his direction. He shook his head. Ben Nicholas emerged from his shop next door and walked toward the bar, slowly and solemnly, moving his lips and paying no attention to the newsman on the steps.

Turning up his coat collar, Qwilleran went to Lombardo's grocery. It was an old-fashioned market with $4.95 Christmas trees heaped on the sidewalk and, inside, a smell of pickles, sausage, and strong cheese. He bought instant coffee and a sweet roll for his breakfast and some round steak and canned consommé for the cats. He also selected some cheese— Cheddar for himself, cream cheese for Yum Yum, and a small wedge of blue for Koko, wondering if the domestic product would be acceptable; Koko was used to genuine Roquefort.

Just as the newsman was leaving the store, the eyes that had been haunting his thoughts all evening materialized in front of him. The blue-white porcelain complexion was wet with snow, and the lashes were spangled with snowflakes. The girl stared and said nothing.

"Well, as you can see, I'm still hanging around the neighborhood," he said to break the silence. "I've moved into the Cobb mansion."

"You have? You really have?" Miss Duckworth's expression brightened, as if living in Junktown constituted an endorsement of character. She pushed her fur hood back from her blue-black hair, now piled in a ballerina's topknot.

"The auction was an interesting experience. A lot of dealers were there, but I didn't see you."

She shook her head wistfully. "I thought of going, but I lacked the courage."

"Miss Duckworth," said Qwilleran, coming boldly to the point, "I'd like to write a tribute to Andy Glanz, but I need more information. I wish you'd fill me in." He could see her shrinking from the suggestion. "I know it's a painful subject for you, but Andy deserves the best we can give him."

She hesitated. "You wouldn't quote me directly, would you?"

"Word of honor!"

"Very well," she said in a small voice, searching Qwilleran's face for reassurance. "When?"

"Sooner the better."

"Would you like to come over to my place tonight?"

"If it isn't too late for you."

"I always stay up half the night." She said it wearily.

"I'll take my groceries home and be right over."

A few minutes later Qwilleran went striding through the snow to The Blue Dragon with an elation that was only partly connected with the Andy Glanz story, and he soon found himself sitting on a stiff velvet sofa in the gold and blue living room and enjoying the aroma of sandalwood furniture wax. The belligerent dog had been penned up in the kitchen.

The girl explained, "My family disapproves of this neighborhood, and they insist I keep Hepplewhite for protection. Sometimes he takes his job too seriously."

"There seems to be a sharp division of opinion about Junktown," said Qwilleran. "Is it really a bad neighborhood?"

"We have no trouble," Miss Duckworth said. "Of course, I observe certain precautions, as any woman should if she lives alone."

She brought a silver coffeepot on a silver tray, and Qwilleran watched her silky movements with admiration. She had the long-legged grace he admired in Koko and Yum Yum. What a sensation she would make at the Press Club on Christmas Eve! he told himself. She was wearing slim, well-fitted trousers in a delectable shade of blue, and a cashmere sweater dyed to match, probably at great expense.

"Have you ever done any fashion modeling?" he asked.

"No." She smiled patiently, as if she had been asked a thousand times before. "But I did a great deal of Modern Dance at Bennington."

She poured one cup of coffee. Then, to Qwilleran's surprise, she reached for a crystal decanter with a silver label and poured Scotch for herself.

He said, "Well, I rented Mrs. Cobb's apartment this afternoon and moved in immediately—with my two roommates, a pair of Siamese cats."

"Really? You hardly look like a man who would keep cats."

Qwilleran eyed her defensively. "They were orphans. I adopted them—first the male and then, some months later, the female."

"I'd like to have a cat," she said. "Cats seem to go with antiques. They're so gentle."

"You don't know Siamese! When they start flying around, you think you've been hit by a Caribbean hurricane."

"Now that you have an apartment, you ought to buy the Mackintosh coat of arms. It would be perfect over your fireplace. Would you like to take it home on approval?"

"It's rather heavy to be lugging back and forth. In fact," Qwilleran said, "I was surprised to see you handle it with so much ease this morning."

"I'm strong. In this business you have to be strong."

"What do you do for recreation? Lift weights?"

She gave a small laugh. "I read about antiques, attend antiques lectures, and go to exhibits at the historical museum."

"You've got it bad, haven't you?"

She looked at him engagingly. "There's something mystic about antiques. It's more than intrinsic value or beauty or age. An object that has been owned and cherished by other human beings for centuries develops a personality of its own that reaches out to you. It's like an old friend. Do you understand? I wish I could make people understand."

"You explain it very well, Miss Duckworth."

"Mary," she said.

"Mary, then. But if you feel so strongly about antiques, why don't you want to share your interest with our readers? Why don't you let me quote you?"

She hesitated. "I'll tell you why," she said suddenly. "It's because of my family. They don't approve of what I'm doing, living on Zwinger Street and peddling—junk!"

"What's their objection?"

"Father is a banker, and bankers are rather stuffy. He's also English. The combination is deadly. He subsidizes my business venture on condition that I don't embarrass the family. That's why I must decline any publicity."

She refilled Qwilleran's coffee cup and poured herself another Scotch.

In a teasing tone he said, "Do you always serve your guests coffee while you drink pedigreed Scotch?"

"Only when they are total abstainers," she replied with a smug smile.

"How did you know I'm on the wagon?"

She buried her nose in her glass for a few seconds. "Because I called my father this afternoon and had him check your credentials. I found out that you've been a crime reporter in New York, Los Angeles, and elsewhere, and that you once wrote an important book on urban crime, and that you've won any number of national journalism awards." She folded her arms and looked triumphant.

Warily Qwilleran said, "What else did you find out?"

"That you had some lean years as a result of an unhappy marriage and a case of alcoholism, but you made a successful recovery, and the *Daily Fluxion* employed you last February, and you have been doing splendidly ever since."

Qwilleran flushed. He was used to prying into the lives of others; it was disconcerting to have his own secrets exposed. "I should be flattered that you're interested," he said with chagrin. "Who is your father? What's his bank?"

The girl was enjoying her moment of oneupmanship. She was also enjoying her drink. She slid down in her chair and crossed her long legs. "Can I trust you?"

"Like a tombstone."

"He's Percival Duxbury. Midwest National."

"Duxbury! Then Duckworth isn't your real name?"

"It's a name I've taken for professional purposes."

Qwilleran's hopes for Christmas Eve soared; a Duxbury would make an impressive date at the Press Club. They immediately crashed; a Duxbury would probably never accept the invitation.

"A Duxbury in Junktown!" he said softly. "That would really make headlines."

"You promised," she reminded him, snapping out of her casual pose.

"I'll keep my promise," he said. "But tell me: why are you doing business on Zwinger Street? A nice shop like this belongs downtown—or in Lost Lake Hills."

"I fell in love," she said with a helpless gesture. "I fell in love with these wonderful old houses. They have so much character and such potential for restoration. At first I was attracted to the idea of a proud old neighborhood resisting modernization, but after I had been here for a few months, I fell in love with the people."

"The antique dealers?"

"Not exactly. The dealers are dedicated and plucky, and I admire them—with certain reservations—but I'm talking about the people on the street. My heart goes out to them—the working

class, the old people, the lonely ones, foreigners, il-
literates, even the shady characters. Are you
shocked?"

"No. Surprised. Pleasantly surprised. I think I
know what you mean. They're earthy; they get to
you."

"They're genuine, and they're unabashed individ-
ualists. They have made my former life seem so su-
perficial and useless. I wish I could do something for
the neighborhood, but I don't know what it would
be. I have no money of my own, and Father made
me promise not to mix."

Qwilleran regarded her with a wishful wonder
that she misinterpreted.

"Are you hungry?" she asked. "I think I'll find us
something to eat."

When she returned with crackers and caviar and
smoked salmon, he said, "You were going to tell me
about Andy Glanz. What kind of man was he? How
did the junkers feel about him?"

The Scotch had relaxed her. She put her head
back, gazed at the ceiling and collected her thoughts,
her posture and trousered legs jarringly out of tune
with the prim eighteenth century room.

"Andy did a great deal for Junktown," she began,
"because of his scholarly approach to antiques. He
gave talks to women's clubs. He convinced the museum curators and the serious collectors to venture
into Zwinger Street."

"Could I call him the major-domo of Junktown?"

"I'd avoid saying that, if I were you. C.C. Cobb

considers himself the neighborhood leader. He opened the first shop and promoted the idea of Junktown."

"How would you describe Andy as to character?"

"Honest—scrupulously honest! Most of us have a little larceny in our hearts, but not Andy! And he had a great sense of responsibility. I saw him make a citizen's arrest one night. We were driving past an abandoned house in the reclamation area, and we saw a light inside. Andy went in and caught a man stripping the plumbing fixtures."

"That's illegal, I assume."

"Condemned houses are city property. Yes, it's technically illegal. Anyone else would have looked the other way, but Andy was never afraid to get involved."

Qwilleran shifted his position on the stiff sofa. "Did the other dealers share your admiration for Andy's integrity?"

"Yes-s-s . . . and no," Mary said. "There's always jealousy among dealers, even though they appear to be the best of friends."

"Did Andy have any other friends I could interview?"

"There's Mrs. McGuffey. She's a retired schoolteacher, and Andy helped her start her antique shop. He was magnanimous in many ways."

"Where would I find the lady?"

"At The Piggin, Noggin and Firkin in the next block."

"Did Andy get along with Cobb?"

She drew a deep breath. "Andy was a diplomat. He knew how to handle C.C."

"Mrs. Cobb was evidently very fond of Andy."

"All women adored him. Men were not so enthusiastic, perhaps. It usually happens that way, doesn't it?"

"How about Ben Nicholas? Did they hit it off?"

"Their relations were amicable, although Andy thought Ben spent too much time at The Lion's Tail."

"Is Ben a heavy drinker?"

"He likes his brandy, but he never gets out of line. He used to be an actor. Every city has one antique dealer who used to be on the stage and one who makes it a point to be obnoxious."

"What do you know about the blond fellow on crutches?"

"Russell Patch used to work for Andy, and they were great friends. Then suddenly they parted company, and Russ opened his own shop. I'm not sure what caused the rift."

"But you were Andy's closest friend?" Qwilleran asked with a searching look.

Abruptly Mary Duckworth stood up and wandered around the room hunting for her cigarette holder. She found it and sat on the sofa and let Qwilleran offer her a light. After one deep inhalation she laid the cigarette down and curled up as if in pain, hugging her knees. "I miss Andy so much," she whispered.

Qwilleran had a desire to reach out and comfort

her, but he restrained himself. He said, "You've had
a shock, and you've been living with your grief. You
shouldn't bottle it up. Why don't you tell me about
it? I mean, everything that happened on that night.
It might do you some good."

The warmth of his tone brought a wetness to her
dark eyes. After a while she said, "The terrible thing
is that we quarreled on our last evening together. I
was feeling peevish. Andy had . . . done
something . . . that irritated me. He was trying to
make amends, but I kept goading him during dinner."

"Where did you have dinner?"

"Here. I made beef Bordelaise, and it was a fail-
ure. The beef was tough, and we had this personal
argument, and at nine o'clock he went back to his
shop. He said someone was coming to look at a
light fixture. Some woman from the suburbs was
bringing her husband to look at a chandelier."

"Did he say he would return?"

"No. He was rather cool when he left. But after
he'd gone, I felt miserable, and I decided to go to his
shop and apologize. That's when I found him—"

"Was his shop open?"

"The back door was unlocked. I went in the back
way—from the alley. Don't ask me to describe what
I saw!"

"What did you do?"

"I don't remember. Iris says I ran to the mansion,
and C.C. called the police. She says she brought me
home and put me to bed. I don't remember."

Intent on their conversation, neither of them heard the low growl in the kitchen—at first no more than a rattle in the dog's throat.

"I shouldn't be telling you this," Mary said.

"It's good to get it off your mind."

"You won't mention it, will you?"

"I won't mention it."

Mary sighed deeply and was quiet, while Qwilleran smoked his pipe and admired her large dark-rimmed eyes. They had mellowed during the evening, and now they were beautiful.

"You were right," she said. "I feel better now. For weeks after it happened, I had a horrible dream, night after night. It was so vivid that I began to think it was true. I almost lost my mind! I thought—"

It was then that the dog barked—in a voice full of alarm.

"Something's wrong," Mary said, jumping to her feet, and her eyes widened to their unblinking stare.

"Let me go and see" Qwilleran said.

Hepplewhite was barking at the rear window.

"There's a police car at the end of the alley," the newsman said. "You stay here. I'll see what it's all about. Is there a rear exit?"

He went down the narrow back stairs and out through a walled garden, but the gate to the alley was padlocked, and he had to return for a key.

By the time he reached the scene, the morgue wagon had arrived, and the revolving roof lights on the two police vehicles made blue flashes across the snow and the faces of a few onlookers and a figure lying on the ground.

Qwilleran stepped up to one of the officers and said, "I'm from the *Daily Fluxion*. What's happened here?"

"Routine lush," said the man in uniform with a smirk. "Drank too much antifreeze."

"Know who he is?"

"Oh, sure. He's got a pocketful of credit cards and a diamond-studded platinum ID bracelet."

Qwilleran moved closer as the body was loaded on a stretcher, and he saw the man's coat. He had seen that coat before.

Mary was waiting for him in the walled garden, and although she was warmly wrapped, she was shaking. "Wh-what was the matter?"

"Just a drunk," he told her. "You'd better get indoors before you catch cold. You're shivering."

They went upstairs, and Qwilleran prescribed hot drinks for both of them.

As Mary warmed her hands on her coffee cup, he studied her face. "You were telling me—just before the dog barked—about your recurrent dream."

She shuddered. "It was a nightmare! I suppose I was feeling guilty because I had been unpleasant to Andy."

"What did you dream?"

"I dreamed . . . I kept dreaming that I had *pushed* Andy to his death on that finial!"

Qwilleran paused before making his comment. "There may be an element of fact in your dream."

"What do you mean?"

"I have a hunch that Andy's death was not an accidental fall from a ladder." As he said it, he again felt the telltale prickling in his moustache.

Mary became defensive. "The police called it an accident."

"Did they investigate? Did they come to see you? They must have inquired who found the body."

She shook her head.

"Did they interview people in the neighborhood?"

"It was not necessary. It was obviously a mishap. Where did you get the idea that it might have been . . . anything else?"

"One of your talkative neighbors—this morning—"

"Nonsense."

"I assumed he must have some reason for calling it murder."

"Just an irresponsible remark. Why would anyone say such a thing?"

"I don't know." Then Qwilleran watched Mary's eyes grow wide as he added, "But by a strange coincidence, the man who told me is now on his way to the morgue."

Whether it was that statement or the startling sound of the telephone bell, he could not tell, but Mary froze in her chair. It rang several times.

"Want me to answer?" Qwilleran offered, glancing at his watch.

She hesitated, then nodded slowly.

He found the phone in the library across the hall.

"Hello? . . . Hello? . . . Hello? . . . They hung up," he reported when he returned to the living room. Then noticing Mary's pallor, he asked, "Have you had this kind of call before? Have you been getting crank calls? Is that why you stay up late?"

"No, I've always been a night owl," she said, shaking off her trance. "My friends know it, and someone was probably phoning to—discuss the late movie on TV. They often do that. Whoever it was undoubtedly hung up because of hearing a man's voice. It would appear that I had company, or it might have seemed to be a wrong number."

She talked too fast and explained too much. Qwilleran was unconvinced.

SEVEN

Qwilleran went home through snow that was ankle-deep, its hush accentuating the isolated sounds of the night: a blast of jukebox music from The Lion's Tail, the whine of an electric motor somewhere, the idle bark of a dog. But first he stopped at the all-night drugstore on the corner and telephoned the *Fluxion*'s night man in the Press Room at Police Headquarters and asked him to check two Dead on Arrivals from the Junktown area.

"One came in tonight and one October sixteenth," Qwilleran said. "Call me back at this number, will you?"

While he was waiting, he ordered a ham sandwich and considered the evidence. The death of the man in a horse-blanket coat might have no significance, but the fear in Mary's eyes was real and incontrovertible, and her emphatic insistence that Andy's death was an accident left plenty of room for conjecture. If it was murder, there had to be motive, and Qwilleran had an increasing curiosity about the young man of superior integrity who made citizen's arrests. He knew the type. On the surface they looked good, but they could be troublemakers.

The phone call came in from the police reporter. "That October DOA was filed as accidental death," he said, "but I couldn't get any dope on the other one. Why don't you try again in the morning?"

Qwilleran went home, tiptoed up the protesting stairs of the Cobb mansion, unlocked his door with the big key, and searched for the cats. They were asleep on their blue cushion on top of the refrigerator, curled together in a single mound of fur with one nose, one tail and three ears. One eye opened and looked at him, and Qwilleran could not resist stroking the pair. Their fur was incredibly silky when they were relaxed, and it always appeared darker when they were asleep.

Soon after, he settled in his own bed, hoping that his mates at the Press Club never found out he was sleeping in a swan boat.

It was then that he heard the odd sound—like soft moaning. It was the purring of cats, but louder. It was the cooing of pigeons, but more guttural. It had a mechanical regularity, and it seemed to be coming from the partition behind his bed—the wall that was papered with book leaves. He listened—keenly at fist, then drowsily, and the monotony of the sound soon lulled him to sleep.

He slept well that first night in the Cobb mansion, dreaming pleasantly of the Mackintosh coat of arms with its three snarling cats and its weathered blues and reds. His pleasurable dreams were always in color; others were in sepia, like old-time rotogravure.

On Saturday morning, as he began to emerge from slumber, he felt a great weight pressing on his chest. In the first stages of waking, before his eyes were open and before his mind was clear, he had a vision of the iron coat of arms, crushing him, pinning him to the bed. He struggled to regain his senses, and as he succeeded in opening his eyelids, he found himself staring into two violet-blue eyes, slightly crossed. Little Yum Yum was sitting on his chest in a compact and featherweight bundle. He took a deep breath of relief, and the heaving of his chest pleased her. She purred. She reached out one velvety paw and touched his moustache tenderly. She used the stubble on his chin to scratch the top of her head.

Then, from somewhere overhead, came an imperious command. Koko was sitting on the tail of the swan, making pronouncements in a loud voice. Either he was ordering breakfast, or he was deploring Yum Yum's familiarity with the man of the house. Koko seemed to have strong ideas about priorities.

The steam was hissing and clanking in the radiators, and when the heat came on in this old house, the whole building smelled of baked potatoes. Qwilleran got up and diced some round steak for the cats and heated it in a spoonful of consommé, while Koko supervised and Yum Yum streaked around the apartment, chased by an imaginary pursuer. For his own breakfast the newsman was contemplating the sugary bun that had become unappetizingly gummy during the night.

As he arranged the diced meat on one of the antique blue and white plates that came with the apartment, he heard a knock on the door. Iris Cobb was standing there, beaming at him.

"I'm sorry. Did I get you out of bed?" she asked when she saw the red plaid bathrobe. "I heard you talking to the cats and thought you were up. Here's a fresh shower curtain for your bathtub. Did you sleep well?"

"Yes, it's a good bed." Qwilleran protruded his lower lip and blew into his moustache, dislodging a cat hair that was waving under his nose.

"I had a terrible night. C.C. snored like a foghorn, and I didn't get a wink of sleep. Is there anything you need? Is everything all right?"

"Everything's fine, except that my toothbrush has disappeared. I put it in a tumbler last night, and this morning it's gone."

Iris rolled her eyes. "It's Mathilda! She's hidden it somewhere. Just hunt around and you'll find it. Would you like a few antique accessories to make your apartment more homey? Some colored glass? Some figurines?"

"No, thanks, but I'd like to get a telephone installed in a hurry."

"You can call the phone company from our apartment. And why don't you let me fix you a bite of breakfast? I made corn muffins for C.C. before he went picketing, and there's half a panful left."

Qwilleran remembered the sticky breakfast roll glued to its limp paper wrapper—and accepted.

Later, while he was eating bacon and eggs and buttering hot corn muffins, Iris talked to him of the antiques business. "You know the dentist's chair that was in your apartment?" she said. "C.C. originally found it in the basement of a clinic that was being torn down, and Ben Nicholas bought it from him for fifty dollars. Then Ben sold it to Andy for sixty dollars. After that, Russ gave Andy seventy-five for it and put new leather on the seat. When C.C. saw it, he wanted it back, so Russ let it go for a hundred and twenty-five, and yesterday we sold it for two hundred and twenty dollars."

"Cozy arrangement," said Qwilleran.

"Don't put that in the paper, though."

"Do all the dealers get along well?"

"Oh, yes. Occasionally there's a flare-up, like the time Andy fired Russ for drinking on the job, but it was soon forgotten. Russ is the one with the gorgeous blond hair. I used to have lovely blond hair myself, but it turned ashen overnight when I lost my first husband. I suppose I should have something done to it."

After breakfast Qwilleran called the telephone

company and asked to have an instrument connected at 6331 Zwinger.

"There will be a fif-ty dol-lar de-pos-it, sir," said the singsong female voice on the line.

"Fifty! In advance! I never heard of such a thing!"

"Sor-ry. You are in zone thir-teen. There is a fif-ty dol-lar de-pos-it."

"What's the zone got to do with it?" Qwilleran shouted into the mouthpiece. "I need that phone immediately, and I'm not going to pay your outrageous deposit! I'm a staff writer for the *Daily Fluxion*, and I'm going to report this to the managing editor."

"One mo-ment, please."

He turned to the landlady. "Of all the high-handed nerve! They want eight months' payment in advance."

"We get that kind of treatment all the time in Junktown," Iris said with a meek shrug.

The voice returned to the line. "Ser-vice will be sup-plied at once, sir. Sor-ry, sir."

Qwilleran was still simmering with indignation when he left the house to cover his beat. He was also unhappy about the loss of his red feather. He was sure it had been in his hatband the night before, but now it was gone, and without it the tweed porkpie lost much of its éclat. A search of the apartment and staircase produced nothing but a cat's hairball and a red gum wrapper.

On Zwinger Street the weather growled at him, and he was in a mood to growl back. All was gray—the sky, the snow, the people. At that moment a white Jaguar sleeked down the street and turned into the carriage house on the block. Qwilleran regarded it as a finger of fate and followed it.

Russell Patch's refinishing shop had been a two-carriage carriage house in its heyday. Now it was half garage and half showroom. The Jaguar shared the space with items of furniture in the last stages of despair—peeling, mildewed, crazed, waterstained, or merely gray with dirt and age—and the premises smelled high of turpentine and lacquer.

Qwilleran heard a scuffing and thumping sound in the back room, and a moment later a husky young man appeared, swinging ably across the rough floor on metal crutches. He was dressed completely in white—white ducks, white open-necked shirt, white socks, white tennis shoes.

Qwilleran introduced himself.

"Yes, I know," said Patch with a smile. "I saw you at the auction, and word got around who you were."

The newsman glanced about the shop. "This is what I call genuine junk-type junk. Do people really buy it?"

"They sure do. It's having a big thing right now. Everything you see here is in the rough; I refinish it to the customer's specifications. See that sideboard? I'll cut off the legs, paint the whole thing mauve, stripe it in magenta, spatter it with umber, and give it a glaze of Venetian bronze. It's going into a two-hundred-thousand-dollar house in Lost Lake Hills."

"How long have you been doing this kind of work?"

"Just six months for myself. Before that, I worked

for Andy Glanz for four years. Want to see how it's done?"

He led the way into the workshop, where he put on a long white coat like a butcher's, daubed with red and brown.

"This rocker," he said, "was sitting out in a barnyard for years. I tightened it up, gave it a red undercoat, and now—watch this." He drew on a pair of plastic gloves and started brushing a muddy substance on the chair seat.

"Did Andy teach you how to do this?"

"No, I picked it up myself," said Patch, with a trace of touchiness.

"From what I hear," Qwilleran said, "he was a great guy. Not only knowledgeable but generous and civic-minded."

"Yeah," the young man said with restraint.

"Everyone speaks highly of him."

Patch made no comment as he concentrated on making parallel brushstrokes, but Qwilleran noticed the muscles of his jaw working.

"His death must have been a great loss to Junktown," the newsman persisted. "Sorry I never had the opportunity to meet—"

"Maybe I shouldn't say this," the refinisher interrupted, "but he was a hard joe to work for."

"How do you mean?"

"Nobody could be good enough to suit Andy."

"He was a perfectionist?"

"He was a professional saint, and he expected everybody to operate the same way. I'm just explaining this because people around here will tell you Andy fired me for drinking on the job, and that's a lie. I quit because I couldn't stand his attitude." Patch gave the red chair seat a final brown swipe and dropped the brush into a tomato can.

"He was sanctimonious?"

"I guess that's the word. I didn't let it get under my skin, you understand. I'm just telling you to keep the record straight. Everybody's always saying how honest Andy was. Well, there's such a thing as being too honest."

"How do you figure that?" Qwilleran asked.

"Okay, I'll explain. Suppose you're driving out in the country, and you see an old brass bed leaning against a barn. It's black, and it's a mess. You knock on the farmhouse door and offer two bucks for it, and most likely they're tickled to have you cart it away. You're in luck, because you can clean it up and make two thousand percent profit. . . . But not Andy! Oh, no, not Andy! If he thought he could peddle the bed for two hundred dollars, he'd offer the farmer a hundred. Operating like that, he was spoiling it for the rest of us." The refinisher's frown changed to a grin. "One time, though, we were out in the country together, and I had the laugh on Andy. The farmer was a real sharpie. He said if Andy was offering a hundred dollars, it must be worth a thousand, and he refused to sell. . . . You want another example? Take scrounging. Everybody scrounges, don't they?"

"What do you mean?"

"You know these old houses that are being torn

down? After a house is condemned, you can go in and find salable things like fireplaces and paneling. So you salvage them before the demolition crew comes along with the wrecking ball."

"Is that legal?"

"Not technically, but you're saving good stuff for someone who can use it. The city doesn't want it, and the wreckers don't give a damn. So we all scrounge once in a while—some more than others. But not Andy! He said a condemned house was city property, and he wouldn't touch it. He wouldn't mind his own business, either, and when he squealed on Cobb, that's when I quit. I thought that was a stinkin' thing to do!"

Qwilleran patted his moustache. "You mean Andy reported Cobb to the authorities?"

Patch nodded. "Cobb got a stiff fine that he couldn't pay, and he would have gone to jail if Iris hadn't borrowed the money. C.C.'s a loud-mouth, but he's not a bad guy, and I thought that was a lousy trick to pull on him. I got a few drinks under my belt and told Andy off."

"Does Cobb know it was Andy who reported him?"

"I don't think anybody knows it was a tip-off. Cobb was prying a staircase out of the Pringle house—he told us all he was going to do it—and the cops came along in a prowl car and nabbed him. It looked like a coincidence, but I happened to hear Andy phoning in an anonymous tip." The refinisher reached for a wad of steel wool and started streaking the sticky glaze on the chair seat. "I have to comb this now—before it sets up too hard," he explained.

"How about Andy's private life?" Qwilleran asked. "Did he have the same lofty standards?"

Russell Patch laughed. "You better ask the Dragon. . . . About this other thing—don't get me wrong. I didn't have any hard feelings against Andy personally, you understand. Some people carry grudges. I don't carry a grudge. I may blow my stack, but then I forget it. You know what I mean?"

After Qwilleran left the carriage house, he made a telephone call from the corner drugstore, where he went to buy a new toothbrush. He called the feature editor at his home.

"Arch," he said, "I've run into an interesting situation in Junktown. You know the dealer who was killed in an accident a couple of months ago—"

"Yes. He's the one who sold me my Pennsylvania tin coffeepot."

"He allegedly fell off a stepladder and allegedly stabbed himself on a sharp object, and I'm beginning to doubt the whole story."

"Qwill, let's not turn this quaint, nostalgic Christmas series into a criminal investigation," the editor said. "The boss wants us to emphasize peace-on-earth and goodwill toward advertisers until the Christmas shopping season is over."

"Just the same, there's something going on in this quaint, nostalgic neighborhood that bears questioning."

"How do you know?"

"Private hunch—and something that happened yesterday. One of the Junktown regulars stopped me on the street and spilled it—that Andy had been murdered."

"Who was he? Who told you that?" Riker demanded.

"Just a neighborhood barfly, but great truths are spoken while under the influence. He seemed to know something, and twelve hours after he talked to me, he was found dead in the alley."

"Drunks are always being found dead in alleys. You should know that."

"There's something else. Andy's girl friend is obviously living in fear. Of what, I can't find out."

"Look, Qwill, why don't you concentrate on writing the antique series and getting yourself a decent place to live?"

"I've got an apartment. I've moved into a haunted house on Zwinger Street—over the Cobb Junkery."

"That's where we bought our dining room chandelier," said Riker. "Now why don't you just relax and enjoy the holidays and—say!—be sure to visit The Three Weird Sisters. You'll flip! When will you have your first piece of copy?"

"Monday morning."

"Keep it happy," Riker advised. "And listen, you donkey! Don't waste any time trying to turn an innocent accident into a Federal case!"

That directive was all the encouragement Qwilleran needed. It was not for nothing that his old friend called him a donkey.

EIGHT

With a stubborn determination to unearth the truth about the death of Andy Glanz, Qwilleran continued his tour of Zwinger Street. He walked past the Bit o' Junk antique shop (closed)—past The Blue Dragon—past a paint store (out of business)—past a bookstore (pornographic)—until he reached a place called Ann's 'Tiques, a subterranean shop smelling of moldy rugs and rotted wood.

The little old white-haired woman seated in a rocking chair resembled a dandelion gone to seed. She looked at Qwilleran blankly and kept on rocking.

"I'm Jim Qwilleran from the *Daily Fluxion*," the newsman said in his courtliest manner.

"Nope, I haven't had one o' them for years," she replied in a reedy voice. "People like the kind with china handles and a double lid."

Qwilleran inspected the litter of indescribable knick-knacks and raised his voice. "What's your specialty, Miss Peabody?"

"No sir! No discounts! If you don't like my prices, leave the things be. Somebody else'll buy 'em."

Qwilleran bowed and left the shop. He walked past a billiard hall (windows boarded up)—past a chili parlor with a ventilator exhausting hot breath across the sidewalk (rancid grease, fried onions, sour mop)—until he reached the fruit and tobacco shack of Papa Popopopoulos. There was an aroma of overripe banana and overheated oil stove in the shack. The proprietor sat on an orange crate, reading a newspaper in his native language and chewing a tobacco-stained moustache of great flamboyance.

Qwilleran stamped his feet and clapped his gloved hands together. "Pretty cold out there," he said.

The man listened attentively. "Tobac?" he said.

Qwilleran shook his head. "No, I just stopped in for a chat. Frankly, that last pouch I bought was somewhat past its prime."

Popopopoulos rose and came forward graciously. "Fruit? Nize fruit?"

"I don't think so. Cozy little place you've got here. How long have you been doing business in Junktown?"

"Pomegranate? Nize pomegranate?" The shop-keeper held up a shriveled specimen with faded red skin.

"Not today," said Qwilleran, looking toward the door.

"Pomegranate make babies!"

Qwilleran made a hasty exit. There was nothing to be learned, he decided, from Andy's two protégés.

It was then that he spotted the shop of The Three Weird Sisters, its window filled with washbowl and pitcher sets, spittoons, and the inevitable spinning wheel. Arch Riker might flip over this junk, but Qwilleran had no intention of flipping. He squared his shoulders and marched into the shop. As soon as he opened the door, his nose lifted. He could smell—was it or wasn't it? Yes, it was—clam chow-der!

Three women wearing orange smocks stopped what they were doing and turned to regard the man with a bushy moustache. Qwilleran returned their gaze. For a moment he was speechless.

The woman sitting at a table addressing Christ-mas cards was a brunette with luscious blue eyes and dimples. The one polishing a brass samovar was a voluptuous orange-redhead with green eyes and a dazzling smile. The young girl standing on a steplad-der hanging ropes of Christmas greens was a tiny blonde with upturned nose and pretty legs.

Qwilleran's face was radiant as he finally man-aged to said, "I'm from the *Daily Fluxion*."

"Yes, we know!" they chorused, and the redhead

added in a husky voice, "We saw you at the auction and *adored* your moustache. Sexiest one we've ever seen in Junktown!" She hobbled toward him with one foot in a walking cast and gave his hand a warm grasp. "Pardon my broken metatarsal. I'm Cluthra. Godawful name, isn't it?"

"And I'm Amberina," the brunette said.

"I've Ivrene," said a chirping voice from the top of the stepladder. "I'm the drudge around here."

The redhead sniffed, "Ivy, the soup's scorching!"

The little blonde jumped down from the ladder and ran into the back room.

Flashing her dimples, the brunette said to Qwilleran, "Would you have a bowl of chowder with us? And some cheese and crackers?"

If they had offered hardtack and goose grease, he would have accepted.

"Let me take your overcoat," said the redhead. "It's awfully warm in here." She threw her smock back over her shoulders, revealing a low-cut neckline and basic architecture of an ample nature.

"Sit here, Mr. Qwilleran." The brunette moved some wire carpet beaters from the seat of a Victorian settee.

"Cigarette?" offered the redhead.

"I'll get you an ashtray," said the brunette.

"I smoke a pipe," Qwilleran told the sisters, groping in his pocket and thinking, If only the guys in the Feature Department could see me now! As he filled his pipe and listened to two simultaneous conversations, he glanced around the shop and saw lead soldiers, cast-iron cherubs, chamber pots, and a tableful of tin boxes that had once held tobacco, crackers, coffee, and the like. The old stenciled labels were half obliterated by rust and scuffmarks, and Qwilleran had an idea. Arch Riker said he collected tin; this was the chance to buy him a crazy Christmas present.

"Do you really sell those old tobacco tins?" he asked. "How much for the little one that's all beat up?"

"We're asking ten," they said, "but if it's for yourself, you can have it for five."

"I'll take it," he said and threw down a nickel, without noticing the expression that passed among them.

The youngest one served the soup in antique shaving mugs. "The Dragon just phoned," she told Qwilleran. "She wants to see you this afternoon." She seemed unduly pleased to give him the message.

"How did she know I was here?"

"Everybody knows everything on this street," the redhead said.

"The Dragon has this place bugged," the young one whispered.

"Ivy, don't talk silly."

The sisters continued the conversation in three-part harmony—Cluthra in her husky voice, Amberina with a musical intonation, and Ivrene piping grace notes from her perch. Eventually Qwilleran brought up the subject of Andy Glanz.

"He was a real guy!" the redhead said with lifted

eyebrows, and her rasping voice showed a trace of tenderness.

"He had quite an intellect, I understand," Qwilleran said.

"Cluthra wouldn't know anything about that," said the young one on the ladder. "She brings out the beast in men."

"Ivy!" came the sharp reprimand.

"It's true, isn't it? You said so yourself."

The brunette hastily remarked, "People don't believe we're sisters. The truth is, we had the same mother but different fathers."

"Does this business support the three of you?"

"Heavens, no! I have a husband, and I do this just for fun. Ivy's still in school—art school—and—"

"And Cluthra lives on her alimony," chipped in the youngest, earning pointed glares from her elders.

"Business has been terrible this month," said the brunette. "Sylvia's the only one who's doing any business around here."

"Who's Sylvia?" Qwilleran asked.

"A rich widow," came the prompt reply from the top of the ladder.

"Sylvia sells camp," the redhead explained.

"That's not what you called it yesterday!" Ivy reminded her.

"Where's her shop?" asked the newsman. "What's her full name?"

"Sylvia Katzenhide. She calls her place Sorta Camp. It's in the next block."

"Cluthra calls her the Cat's Backside," Ivy said, ignoring the exasperated sighs from her sisters.

"If you go to see Sylvia, wear earmuffs," the red-head advised.

"Sylvia's quite a talker," said the brunette.

"She's got verbal diarrhea," said the blonde.

"Ivy!"

"Well, that's what you *said!*"

When Qwilleran left the Three Weird Sisters, he was walking with a light step. He had heard little Ivy say, as he walked out the door, "Isn't he groovy?"

He preened his moustache, undecided whether to answer Mary Duckworth's summons or visit the loquacious Sylvia Katzenhide. Mrs. McGuffey was also on his list, and sooner or later he would like to talk to the outspoken Ivy again—alone. She was a brat, but brats could be useful, and she was an engaging brat, as brats went.

On Zwinger Street a hostile sun had penetrated the winter haze—not to warm the hearts and frozen nosetips of Junktown residents, but to convert the lovely snow into a greasy slush for the skidding of cars and splashing of pedestrians, and Qwilleran's mind went to Koko and Yum Yum—lucky cats, asleep on their cushions, warm and well-fed, with no weather to weather, no deadlines to meet, no decisions to make. It had been a long time since he had consulted Koko, and now he decided to give it a try.

There was a game they played with the unabridged dictionary. The cat dug his claws into the book, and Qwilleran opened to the page indicated, where the catchwords at the top of the columns usually offered some useful clue. Incredible? Yes. But it had worked in the past. A few months before, Qwilleran had been credited with finding a stolen jade collection, but the credit belonged chiefly to Koko and Noah Webster. Perhaps the time had come to play the game again.

He went home and unlocked his apartment door, but neither cat was anywhere in sight. Someone had been in the apartment, though. Qwilleran noticed a slight rearrangement and the addition of several useless gimcracks. The brass candlesticks on the mantel, which he liked, had gone, and in their place stood a pottery pig with a surly sneer.

He called the cats by name and got no answer. He searched the apartment, opening all doors and drawers. He got down on his knees at the fireplace and looked up the chimney. It was an unlikely possibility, but one could never tell about cats!

While he was posed on all fours with his head in the fireplace and his neck twisted in an awkward position, Qwilleran sensed movement in the room behind him. He withdrew his head just in time to see the missing pair walk nonchalantly across the carpet, Koko a few paces ahead of Yum Yum as usual. They had come from nowhere, as cats have a way of doing, holding aloft their exclamatory tails. This unpredictable pair could walk on little cat feet, silent as fog, or they could thump across the floor like clodhoppers.

"You rascals!" Qwilleran said.

"Yow?" said Koko with an interrogative inflection that seemed to imply, "Were you calling us? What's for lunch?"

"I searched all over! Where the devil were you hiding?"

They had come, it seemed, from the direction of the bathroom. They were blinking. Their eyes were intensely blue. And Yum Yum was carrying a toothbrush in her tiny V-shaped jaws. She dropped it in front of him.

"Good girl! Where did you find it?"

She looked at him with eyes bright, crossed, and uncomprehending.

"Did you find it under the tub, sweetheart?"

Yum Yum sat down and looked pleased with herself, and Qwilleran stroked her tiny head without noticing the faraway expression in Koko's slanted eyes.

"Come on, Koko, old boy!" he said. "Let's play the game." He slapped the cover of the dictionary—the starting signal—and Koko hopped on the big book and industriously sharpened his claws on its tattered binding. Then he hopped down and went to the window to watch pigeons.

"The game! Remember the game? Play the game!" Qwilleran urged, opening the book and demonstrating the procedure with his fingernails. Koko ignored the invitation; he was too busy observing the action outdoors.

The newsman grabbed him about the middle and

placed him on the open pages. "Now dig, you little monkey!" But Koko stood there with his back rigidly arched and gave Qwilleran a look that could only be described as insulting.

"All right, skip it!" the man said with disappointment. "You're not the cat you used to be. Go back to your lousy pigeons," and Koko returned his attention to the yard below where Ben Nicholas was scattering crusts of bread.

Qwilleran left the apartment to continue his rounds, and as he went downstairs, Iris Cobb came flying out of the Junkery.

"Are you having fun in Junktown?" she asked gaily.

"I'm unearthing some interesting information," he replied, "and I'm beginning to wonder why the police never investigated Andy's death. Didn't the detectives ever come around asking questions?"

She was shaking her head vaguely when a man's gruff voice from within the shop shouted, "I'll tell you why they didn't. Junktown's a slum, and who cares what happens in a slum?"

Mrs. Cobb explained in a low voice, "My husband is rabid on the subject. He's always feuding with City Hall. Of course, he's probably right. The police would be glad to label it an accident and close the case. They can't be bothered with Junktown." Then her expression perked up; she had the face of a woman who relishes gossip. "Why were you asking about the detectives? Do you have any *suspicions?*"

"Nothing definite, but it was almost too freakish to dismiss as an accident."

"Maybe you're right. Maybe there was something going on that nobody knows about." She shivered. "The idea gives me goosebumps. . . . By the way, I sold the brass candlesticks from your apartment, but I've given you a Sussex pig—very rare. The head comes off, and you can drink out of it."

"Thanks," said Qwilleran.

He started down the front steps and halted abruptly. That toothbrush that Yum Yum had brought him! It had a blue handle, and the handle of his old toothbrush, he seemed to recall, was green. . . . Or was it?

NINE

Qwilleran walked to The Blue Dragon with a long stride, remembering the vulnerable Mary of the night before, but he was greeted by another Mary—the original one—aloof and inscrutable in her Japanese kimono. She was alone in the shop. She sat in her carved teakwood chair, as tall and straight as the wisp of smoke ascending from her cigarette.

"I got your message," he said, somewhat dismayed at the chilly reception. "You *did* say you wanted to see me, didn't you?"

"Yes. I am very much disturbed." She laid down the long cigarette holder and faced him formally.

"What's the trouble?"

"I used poor judgment last night. I am afraid," she said in her precise way, "that I talked too much."

"You were delightful company. I enjoyed every minute."

"That's not what I mean. I should never have revealed my family situation."

"You have nothing to be afraid of. I gave you my word."

"I should have remembered the trick your Jack Jaunti played on my father, but unfortunately the Scotch I was drinking—"

"You were completely relaxed. It was good for you. Believe me, I would never take advantage of your confidence."

Mary Duckworth gave him a penetrating look. There was something about the man's moustache that convinced people of his sincerity. Other moustaches might be villainous or supercilious or pathetic, but the outcropping on Qwilleran's upper lip inspired trust.

Mary took a deep breath and softened slightly. "I believe you. Against my will I believe you. It's merely that—"

"Now may I sit down?"

"I'm sorry. How rude of me. Please make yourself comfortable. May I offer you a cup of coffee?"

"No, thanks. I've just had soup at The Three Weird Sisters."

"Clam chowder, I suppose," said Mary with a

slight curl of the lip. "The shop always reminds me of a fish market."

"It was very good chowder."

"Canned, of course."

Qwilleran sensed rivalry and was inwardly pleased. "Any bad dreams last night?" he asked.

"No. For the first time in months I was able to sleep well. You were quite right. I needed to talk to someone." She paused and looked in his eyes warmly, and her words were heartfelt. "I'm grateful, Qwill."

"Now that you're feeling better," he said, "would you do something for me? Just to satisfy my curiosity?"

"What do you want?" She was momentarily wary.

"Would you give me a few more details about the night of the accident? It's not morbid interest, I assure you. Purely intellectual curiosity."

She bit her lip. "What else can I tell you? I've given you the whole story."

"Would you draw me a diagram of the room where you discovered the body?" He handed her a ball-point pen and a scrap of paper from his pocket—the folded sheet of newsprint that was his standard equipment. Then he knocked his pipe on an ashtray and went through the process of filling and lighting.

Mary gave him a skeptical glance and started to sketch slowly. "It was in the workroom—at the rear of Andy's shop. The back door is here," she said.

"To the right is a long workbench with pigeonholes and hangers for tools. Around the edge of the room Andy had furniture or other items, waiting to be glued or refinished or polished."

"Including chandeliers?"

"They were hanging overhead—perhaps a dozen of them. Lighting fixtures were Andy's specialty."

"And where was the stepladder?"

"In the middle of the room there was a cleared space—about fifteen feet across. The stepladder was off to one side of this area." She marked the spot with an X. "And the crystal chandelier was on the floor nearby—completely demolished."

"To the right or left of the ladder?"

"To the right." She made another X.

"And the position of the body?"

"Just to the left of the stepladder."

"Face down?"

She nodded.

Qwilleran drew long and slowly on his pipe. "Was Andy right-handed or left-handed?"

Mary stiffened with suspicion. "Are you sure the newspaper didn't send you to pry into this incident?"

"The *Fluxion* couldn't care less. All my paper wants is an entertaining series on the antiquing scene. I guess I spent too many years on the crime beat. I've got a compulsion to check everything out."

The girl studied his sober gaze and the downcurve of the ample moustache, and her voice became tender. "You miss your former work, don't you, Qwill? I suppose antiques seem rather mild after the excitement you've been accustomed to."

"It's an assignment," he said with a shrug. "A newsman covers the story without weighing the psychic rewards."

Her eyes flickered downward. "Andy was right-handed," she said after a moment's pause. "Does it make any difference?"

Qwilleran studied her sketch. "The stepladder was here . . . and the broken chandelier was over here. And the finial, where he fell, was . . . to the left of the ladder?"

"Yes."

"In the middle of the floor? That was a strange place for a lethal object like that."

"Well, it was—toward the edge of the open space—with the other items that had been pushed back around the walls."

"Had you seen it there before?"

"Not exactly in that location. The finial, like everything else, moved about frequently. The day before the accident it was on the workbench. Andy was polishing the brass ball."

"Was it generally known that he owned the finial?"

"Oh, yes. Everyone assured him he had bought a white elephant. Andy quipped that some fun-type suburbanite would think it was a fun thing for serving pretzels."

"How did he acquire it in the first place? The auctioneer said it came from an old house that had been torn down."

"Andy bought it from Russell Patch. Russ is a great scrounger. In fact, that's how he fractured his leg. He and Cobb were stripping an empty house, and Russ slipped off the roof."

"Let me get this straight," Qwilleran said. "Andy didn't believe in scrounging, and yet he was willing to buy from scroungers? Technically that finial was hot merchandise."

Mary's shrug was half apology for Andy and half rebuke for Qwilleran.

He smoked his pipe in silence and wondered about this girl who was disarmingly candid one moment and wary the next—lithe as a willow and strong as an oak—masquerading under an assumed name—absolutely sure of certain details and completely blank about others—alternately compassionate and aloof.

After a while he said, "Are you perfectly satisfied that Andy's death was accidental?"

There was no response from the girl—merely an unfathomable stare.

"It might have been suicide."

"No!"

"It might have been attempted robbery."

"Why don't you leave well enough alone?" Mary said, fixing Qwilleran with her wide-eyed gaze. "If rumors start circulating, Junktown is bound to suffer. Do you realize this is the only neighborhood in town that's been able to keep down crime? Customers still feel safe here, and I want to keep it that way." Then her tone turned bitter. "I'm a fool, of course, for thinking we have a future. The city wants to tear all of this down and build sterile high-rise apartments. Meanwhile, we're designated as a slum, and the banks refuse to lend money to property owners for improvements."

"How about your father?" Qwilleran asked. "Does he subscribe to this official policy?"

"He considers it entirely reasonable. You see, no one thinks of Junktown as a community of living people—merely a column of statistics. If they would ring doorbells, they would find respectable foreign families, old couples with no desire to move to the suburbs, small businessmen like Mr. Lombardo—all nationalities, all races, all ages, all types—including a certain trashy element that does no harm. That's the way a city should be—one big hearty stew. But politicians have an à la carte mentality. They refuse to mix the onions and carrots with the tenderloin tips."

"Has anyone tried to fight it?"

"C.C. has made a few attempts, but what can one man accomplish?"

"With your name and your influence, Mary, you could get something done."

"Dad would never hear of it! Not for a minute! Do you know how I am classified at the Licensing Bureau? As a junk dealer! The newspapers would have a field day with *that* item. . . . Do you see that Chippendale chair near the fireplace? It's priced two thousand dollars! But I'm licensed as a Class C junk dealer."

"Someone should organize this whole community," Qwilleran said.

"You're undoubtedly right. Junktown has no voice at City Hall." She walked to the bay window. "Look at those refuse receptacles! In every other part of town the rubbish is collected in the rear, but Junktown's alleys are too narrow for the comfort of the city's 'disposal engineers,' and they require us to put those ugly containers on the sidewalk. Thursday is collection day; this is Saturday, and the rubbish is still there."

"The weather has fouled everything up," Qwilleran said.

"You talk like a bureaucrat. Excuses! That's all we hear."

Qwilleran had followed her to the window. The street was indeed a sorry sight. "Are you sure Junktown has a low crime rate?" he asked.

"The antique dealers never have any trouble. And I'm not afraid to go out at night, because there are always people of one sort or another walking up and down the street. Some of my rich customers in the suburbs are afraid to drive into their own garages!"

The newsman looked at Mary with new respect. Abruptly he said, "Are you free for dinner tonight, by any chance?"

"I'm dining with my family," she said with regret. "Mother's birthday. But I appreciate your invitation." Then she took a small silvery object from the drawer of a secretary-desk and slipped it into Qwilleran's hand. "Souvenir of Junktown," she said. "A tape measure. I give them to my customers because they always want to know the height, width, depth, length, diameter, circumference, and thickness of everything they see."

Qwilleran glanced toward the rear of the shop. "I notice nobody's bought the Mackintosh coat of arms." He refrained from mentioning that he had dreamed about it.

"It's still there, pining for you. I think you were made for each other. When the right customer meets the right antique, something electric happens—like falling in love. I can see sparks between you and that piece of iron."

He gave her a quick glance; she was quite serious. He tugged at his moustache, reflecting that one hundred twenty-five dollars would buy him two suits of clothes.

She said, "You don't need to pay for it until after Christmas. Why don't you take it home and enjoy it over the holidays? It's just gathering dust here."

"All right!" he said with sudden resolve. "I'll give you a twenty-dollar deposit."

He rolled the hoop-shaped coat of arms to the front door.

"Can you manage it alone? Why don't you ask C.C. to help you carry it up to your apartment?" she suggested. "And don't drop it on your toe," she called out, as Qwilleran struggled down the front steps with his burden.

When he and his acquisition reached the foyer of the Cobb mansion, he stopped to catch his breath, and he heard the ranting voice of C.C. coming from The Junkery.

"You don't know a piece of black walnut from a hole in your head!" Cobb was saying. "Why don't you admit it?"

"If that's black walnut, I'll eat my crutch. You're the biggest fake in the business! I'll give you twenty bucks—no more!"

Qwilleran wrestled the ironwork up the staircase alone.

The cats were asleep in the Morris chair, curled up like Yin and Yang, and Qwilleran did not disturb them. He leaned the coat of arms against the wall and left the apartment, hoping to make three more stops before calling it a day. He had promised to visit Ben's shop, but first he wanted to meet the talkative Sylvia Katzenhide. He liked garrulous subjects; they made his job so easy.

Arriving at The Sorta Camp shop, he held the door open for a well-dressed man who was leaving with a large purchase wrapped in newspaper, black tubes protruding from the wrappings. Inside the shop a woman customer was haggling over the price of a chair made out of automobile tires.

"My dear," Sylvia was telling her, "age and intrinsic value are unimportant. Camp is all wit and whimsy, plus a gentle thumbing of the nose. Either you dig it or you don't, as my son would say."

Mrs. Katzenhide was a handsome, well-groomed, self-assured woman who looked forty and was undoubtedly fifty-five. Qwilleran had seen hundreds like her in the women's auxiliary at the art museum, all identical in their well-cut tweed suits, jersey blouses, gold chains, and alligator shoes. This one had added black cotton stockings as a touch of eccentricity that seemed to be necessary in Junktown.

Qwilleran introduced himself and said, "Was I seeing things, or did a man leave this store with a stuffed—"

"You're right! A stuffed octopus," said Mrs. Katzenhide. "Hideous thing! I was glad to get rid of it. That was Judge Bennett from Municipal Court. Do you know the judge? He bought the octopus for his wife's Christmas present. She's mad about crawly things."

"How come you're dealing in—"

"In camp? It was my son's idea. He said I needed a project to keep my mind off myself." She lighted a cigarette. "Did you know my late husband? He was corporation counsel for the city. My son is in law school. . . . Excuse me, would you like a cigarette?"

Qwilleran declined. "But why camp? Why not something more—"

"More genteel? that's what all my friends say. But you have to *know something* to deal in genuine antiques. Besides, my son insists that camp is what the public wants. If anything is unattractive, poorly made, and secondhand, it sells like hot cakes. I really don't understand it."

"Then I suppose you didn't buy anything at—"

"At the auction yesterday?" The woman had a phenomenal knack for reading minds. "Just a small chandelier for my own apartment. When my husband passed away, I gave up the big house in Lost Lake Hills and moved to Skyline Towers. I have a lovely apartment, and it's not furnished in camp, believe me!"

"How do the Junktown dealers regard your specialty? Have you—"

"Developed a rapport? Definitely! I go to their association meetings, and we get along beautifully. When I first opened the shop, Andrew Glanz took me under his wing and gave me a lot of valuable advice." She heaved a great sigh. "It was a shock to lose that boy. Did you know Andy?"

"No, I never met him. Was he—?"

"Well, I'll tell you. He always gave the impression of wearing a white tie and tails, even when he was in dungarees and scraping down a piece of furniture. And he was so good-looking—and intelligent. I always thought it was a pity he never married. What a waste!"

"Wasn't he more or less engaged to—"

"The Dragon? Not in the formal sense, but they would have made a perfect couple. Too bad he had to get mixed up with that other woman."

"You mean . . ." said Qwilleran with an encouraging pause.

"Here I am, prattling again! My son says I've become an incorrigible gossip since coming to Junktown. And he's right. I'm not going to say another word."

And she didn't.

There were obvious disadvantages to Qwilleran's position. He was trying to investigate an incident that no one wanted him to investigate, and he was not even sure what he was investigating. Any sensible man would have dropped the matter.

Stroking his moustache thoughtfully, Qwilleran took the next step in his noninvestigation of a questionable crime; he visited the shop called Bit o' Junk, a choice that he later regretted.

TEN

Bit o' Junk was next door to the Cobb Junkery, sharing the block with The Blue Dragon, Russell Patch's carriage house, Andy's place on the corner, and a variety store that catered to the needs of the community with embroidered prayer books and black panties trimmed with red fringe. Ben had his shop on the main floor of a town house that was similar in design to the Cobb mansion, but only half as wide and twice as dilapidated. The upper floors were devoted to sleeping rooms for men only, according to a weather-stained sign on the building.

Qwilleran climbed the icy stone steps and entered

a drab foyer. Through the glass panes of the parlor doors he could see a hodge-podge of cast-offs: dusty furniture, unpolished brass and copper, cloudy glass, and other dreary oddments. The only thing that attracted him was the kitten curled up on a cushion with chin on paw. It was in the center of a table full of breakables, and Qwilleran could imagine with what velvet-footed care the small animal had tiptoed between the goblets and teacups. He went in.

At the sight of the bushy moustache, the proprietor rose from a couch and extended his arms in melodramatic welcome. Ben was wearing a bulky ski sweater that emphasized his rotund figure, and with it he sported a tall silk hat. He swept off the hat and bowed low.

"How's business? Slow?" Qwilleran asked as he appraised the unappealing shop.

"Weary, stale, flat, and unprofitable," said the dealer, returning the hat to cover his thinning hair.

Qwilleran picked up a World War I gas mask.

"An historic treasure," Nicholas informed him. "Came over on the *Mayflower*." He padded after the newsman in white stockinged feet.

"I hear you used to be in the theatre," the newsman remarked.

The tubby little dealer drew himself up from five-feet-four to five-feet-five. "Our Friar Laurence on Broadway was acclaimed by critics. Our Dogberry was superb. Our Bottom was unforgettable. . . . How now? You tremble and look pale!"

Qwilleran was staring at the kitten on its cushion. "That—that cat!" he sputtered. "It's dead!"

"An admirable example of the taxidermist's art. You like it not?"

"I like it not," said Qwilleran, and he blew into his moustache. "What's your specialty, anyway? Do you have a specialty?"

"I am a merry wanderer of the night."

"Come off it. You don't have to put on a performance for me. If you want any publicity, give me some straight answers. Do you specialize in anything?"

Ben Nicholas pondered. "Anything that will turn a profit."

"How long have you been operating in Junktown?"

"Too long."

"Did you know Andy Glanz very well?"

The dealer folded his hands and rolled his eyes upward. "Noble, wise, valiant, and honest," he intoned. "It was a sad day for Junktown when Saint Andrew met his untimely end." Then he hitched his trousers and said roguishly, "How about a tankard of sack at the local pub?"

"No, thanks. Not today," said Qwilleran. "What's this? A folding bookrack?" He had picked up a hinged contraption in brassbound ebony. "How much do you want for it?"

"Take it—take it—with the compliments of jolly old St. Nicholas."

"No, I'll buy it if it isn't too expensive."

"We have been asking fifteen, but allow us to extend the favor of a clergyman's discount. Eight simoleons."

At this point another customer, who had entered the shop and had been thoroughly ignored, said impatiently, "Got any horse brasses?"

"Begone, begone!" said the dealer, waving the man away. "This gentlemen is from the press, and we are being interviewed."

"I'm through. I'm leaving," said the newsman. "I'll send a photographer Monday to get a picture of you and your shop," and he paid for the bookrack.

"I humbly thank you, sir."

Nicholas doffed his silk topper and held it over his heart, and that was when Qwilleran noticed the small red feather stuck in the hat. It was *his feather!* There was no doubt about it; it had a perforation near the quill. In a playful moment two weeks before, he had plucked it from his hatband to tickle Koko's nose, but the cat's jaws were faster than the man's hand, and Koko had punctured the feather with the snap of a fang.

Qwilleran walked slowly from the shop. He stood at the top of the stone steps, wondering how that feather had made its way to Ben's topper.

As he stood there, frowning, Qwilleran was suddenly struck down. All creation descended on him, and he fell to his knees on the stone stoop. There was a rush and a roar and a crash, and he was down on hands and knees in snow and ice.

In a matter of seconds Ben Nicholas came rushing

to his aid. "A bloody avalanche!" he cried, helping the newsman to his feet. "From the roof of this benighted establishment! We shall sue the landlord."

Qwilleran brushed the snow from his clothes. "Lucky I was wearing a hat," he said.

"Come back and sit down and have a wee drop of brandy."

"No, I'm okay. Thanks just the same."

He picked up his bookrack and started down the stone steps, favoring his left knee.

When Qwilleran reached his apartment, having ascended the stairs with difficulty, he was greeted by a rampaging Koko. While Yum Yum sat on the bookcase with her shoulder blades up, looking like a frightened grasshopper, Koko raced from the door to the desk, then up on the daybed and back to the roll-top desk.

"So! Those monkeys installed my phone!" Qwilleran said. "I hope you bit the phone company's representative on the ankle."

Koko watched with interest and wigwagging ears while Qwilleran dialed the *Fluxion* Photo Lab and requisitioned a photographer for Monday morning. Then the cat led the way into the kitchen with exalted tail and starched gait to supervise the preparation of his dinner. With his whiskers curved down in anticipation, he sat on the drainboard and watched the chopping of chicken livers, the slow cooking in butter, the addition of cream, and the dash of curry powder.

"Koko, I've joined the club," the man told him.

"The landlady has a wrenched back, Russ Patch has a broken leg, the redhead's in a cast, and now I've got a busted knee! I won't be cutting any rugs at the Press Club tonight."

"Yow," said Koko in a consoling tone.

Qwilleran always spent Saturday evenings at the Press Club, most recently in the company of a young woman who wrote with brown ink, but she was out of the picture now. On a bold chance he looked up The Three Weird Sisters in the phone book and dialed their number. Most women, he was aware, jumped at the chance to dine at the Press Club. Unfortunately, there was no answer at the antique shop.

He then called a girl who worked in the Women's Department at the *Fluxion*—one of the society writers.

"Wish I could," she said, "but I've got to address Christmas cards tonight if I want them to be delivered before New Year's."

"While I have you on the line," he said, "tell me what you know about the Duxbury family."

"They do their bit socially, but they avoid publicity. Why?"

"Do they have any daughters?"

"Five—all named after English queens. All married except one. She came out ten years ago and . . ."

"And what?"

"Went right back in, I guess. You never see her—or hear of her."

"What's her name?"

"Mary. She's the oddball of the family."

"Thanks," said Qwilleran. He went to the Press Club alone.

The club occupied the only old building in the downtown area that had escaped the wrecking ball. A former county jail, it was built like a medieval fortress with turrets, crenelated battlements, and arrow slots. Whenever the city proposed to condemn it for an expressway or civic mall, a scream of outrage went up from the *Daily Fluxion* and the *Morning Rampage*, and no elected or appointed official had dared to campaign against the wrath of the united press.

As Qwilleran limped up the steps of the dismal old building, he met Lodge Kendall, a police reporter, on his way out.

"Come on back, and I'll buy you a drink," Qwilleran said.

"Can't, Qwill. Promised my wife we'd shop for a Christmas tree tonight. If you don't pick one out early, you're out of luck. I hate a lopsided tree."

"Just one question, then. What section of town has the highest crime rate?"

"It's a tossup between the Strip and Sunshine Gardens. Skyline Park is getting to be a problem, too."

"How about Zwinger Street?"

"I don't hear much about Zwinger Street."

"I've taken an apartment there."

"You must be out of your mind! That's a slum."

"Actually it's not a bad place to live."

"Well, don't unpack all your gear—because the city's going to tear it down," Kendall said cheerfully as he departed.

Qwilleran filled a dinner plate at the buffet and carried it to the bar, which was surprisingly vacant. "Where's everybody?" he asked Bruno, the bartender.

"Christmas shopping. Stores are staying open till nine."

"Ever do any junking, Bruno? Are you a collector?" the newsman asked. The bartender was known for his wide range of interests.

"Oh, sure! I collect swizzle sticks from bars all over the country. I've got about ten thousand."

"That's not what I mean. I'm talking about antiques. I just bought part of an iron gate from a castle in Scotland. It's probably been around for three centuries."

Bruno shook his head. "That's what I don't like about antiques. Everything's so *old*."

Qwilleran finished eating and was glad to go home to Junktown, where there were more vital interests than lopsided Christmas trees and swizzle sticks. No one at the Press Club had even noticed he was limping.

On the steps of the Cobb mansion he looked up at the mansard roof punctuated by attic windows. Its slope still held its load of snow. So did the roof of Mary's house. Only Ben's building, though of identical style, had produced an avalanche.

In his apartment Qwilleran found the cats presiding on their gilded thrones with a nice understanding of protocol; Yum Yum as always on Koko's left. The man cut up the slice of ham he had brought them from the Press Club buffet, then went to the typewriter and worked on the Junktown series. After a while Koko jumped on the tavern table and watched the new mechanical contraption in operation—the type flying up to hit the paper, the carriage jerking across the machine. And when Qwilleran stopped to allow a thought to jell, Koko rubbed his jaw against a certain button and reset the margin.

There were two other distractions that evening. There was an occasional thumping and scraping overhead, and there were tantalizing smells drifting across the hall—first anise, then a rich buttery aroma, then chocolate.

Eventually he heard his name called outside his door, and he found the landlady standing there, holding a large brass tray.

"I heard you typing and thought you might like a snack," she said. "I've been doing my Christmas baking." On her tray were chocolate brownies, a china coffee service, and two cups.

Qwilleran was irked at the interruption, but mesmerized by the sight of the frosted chocolate squares topped with walnut halves, and before he could reply, Mrs. Cobb had bustled into the room.

"I've spent the whole evening over a hot stove," she announced. "All the dealers are upstairs making plans for the Christmas Block Party. C.C. has the third floor fixed up kind of cute for meetings. He calls it Hernia Heaven. You known, antique dealers are always—Oh, my! You're limping! What happened?"

"Bumped my knee."

"You must be careful! Knees are pesky things," she warned him. "You sit in the Morris chair and put your leg up on the ottoman, and I'll put the goodies on the tea table between us." She plopped her plumpness into the rocking chair made of bent twigs, unaware that Koko was watching critically from the mantelshelf.

For someone who had spent several hours slaving in the kitchen, Iris Cobb was rather festively attired. Her hair was carefully coifed. She wore a bright pink dress, embroidered with a few sad glass beads, and her two dangling pairs of eyeglasses, one of which was studded with rhinestones.

Qwilleran bit into a rich, dark chocolate square— soft and still warm from the oven and filled with walnut meats—while Mrs. Cobb rocked industriously in the twiggy rocking chair.

"I wanted to talk to you about something," she said. "What I said about Andy's horoscope—I really wasn't serious. I mean I never actually thought there was anything in it. I wouldn't want to stir up any trouble."

"What kind of trouble?"

"Well, I just heard that you're a crime reporter, and I thought you might be here to—"

"That's ancient history," Qwilleran assured her. "Who told you?"

"The Dragon. I went over to borrow some beeswax, and she told me you were a famous crime reporter in New York or somewhere, and I thought you might be here to snoop around. I honestly never thought Andy's fall was anything but a misstep on that ladder, and I was afraid you might get the wrong idea."

"I see," said Qwilleran. "Well, don't worry about it. I haven't had an assignment on the crime beat in a dog's age."

"That's a load off my mind," she said, and she relaxed and began to survey the apartment with a proprietary air.

"Do you care for that papered wall?" she asked with a critical squint. "It would drive me crazy to lie in bed and look at all those printed pages from books. They're applied with peelable paste, so you can pull them off if you object—"

"To tell the truth, I rather like that wall," Qwilleran said as he helped himself to a second chocolate brownie. "It's *Don Quixote* mixed with Samuel Pepys."

"Well, everyone to his own taste. Are you going away for Christmas? I'll be glad to look after the cats."

"No. No plans."

"Do you have a Christmas party at the office?"

"Just a Christmas Eve affair at the Press Club."

"You must have a very interesting job!" She

stopped rocking and looked at him with frank admiration.

"Koko!" Qwilleran shouted. "Stop tormenting Yum Yum." Then he added to Mrs. Cobb, "They're both neutered, but Koko sometimes behaves in a suspicious way."

The landlady giggled and poured another cup of coffee for him. "If you're going to be alone for Christmas," she said, "you must celebrate with us. C.C. trims a big tree, and my son comes here from St. Louis. He's sort of an architect. His father—my first husband—was a schoolteacher. I'm an English major myself, although you'd never guess it. I never read any more. In this business you don't have time for anything. We've had this house four years, and there's always something—"

She prattled on, and Qwilleran wondered abut this fatuous little woman. As a newsman, he was used to being cajoled and plied with food—the latter being one of the fringe benefits of the profession—but he would have preferred a landlady who was a degree less chummy, and he hoped she would leave before the dealers came down from Hernia Heaven.

Her overtures were innocent enough, he was sure. Her exuberance was simply a lack of taste. She was not amply endowed with gray matter, and her attempt to reverse herself about Andy's accident was pathetically transparent. Had she guessed that her husband might be implicated, if it proved to be murder?

"He died of food poisoning—a rare botulism," Mrs. Cobb was saying.

"Who?" asked Qwilleran.

"My first husband. I knew something tragic was going to happen. I'd seen it in his hand. I used to read palms—just as a hobby, you know. Would you like me to read your palm?"

"I don't have much faith in palmistry," Qwilleran said, beginning to edge out of the deep-cushioned Morris chair.

"Oh, be a sport! Let me read your future. I won't tell you if it's anything really bad. You don't have to move an inch. You sit right where you are, and I'll perch on the ottoman."

She plumped her round hips down beside his propped foot and gave his leg a cordial pat, then reached for his hand. "Your right hand, please." She held it in a warm moist grasp and stroked the palm a few times to straighten the curled and uncooperative fingers.

Trapped in the big chair, he wriggled uncomfortably and tried to devise a tactful escape.

"A very interesting palm," she said, putting on one pair of glasses.

She was stroking his hand and bending her head close to study the lines when the room exploded in a frenzy of snarling and soprano screams. Koko had pounced on Yum Yum with a savage growl. Yum Yum shrieked and fought back. They rolled over and over, locked in a double stranglehold.

Mrs. Cobb jumped up. "Heavens! They'll kill each other!"

Qwilleran yelled, smacked his hands at them, struggled to his feet and whacked the nearest cat's rump. Koko gave a nasty growl, and Yum Yum broke away. Immediately Koko gave chase. The little female went up over the desk, round the Morris chair, under the tea table—with Koko in pursuit. Round and round the room they went, with Qwilleran shouting and Mrs. Cobb squealing. On the fourth lap of the flying circus, Yum Yum ducked under the tea table and Koko sailed over it. Qwilleran made a lucky grab for the coffee pot, but Koko skidded on the tray and sent the cream and sugar flying.

"The rug!" the landlady cried. "Get a towel, quick! I'll get a sponge."

She ran from the apartment just as the dealers came hurrying down from Hernia Heaven.

"What's the uproar?" they said. "Who's getting murdered?"

"Only a family quarrel," Qwilleran explained, jerking his head toward the cats.

Koko and Yum Yum were sitting quietly in the Morris chair together. She was looking sweet and contented, and Koko was licking her face with affection.

ELEVEN

Cobb snored again that night. Qwilleran, waked at three o'clock by the pain in his knee, took some aspirin and then listened to the muffled snorts coming through the wall. He wished he had an ice pack. He wished he had never moved to Junktown. The whole community was accident prone, and it seemed to be contagious. Why had he paid a month's rent in advance? No matter; he could stay long enough to complete the Junktown series and then move out, chalking it up to experience: Beware of prospective landladies who give you homemade apple pie. Yes, that was the smart thing to do—concentrate on writing a good series and quit snooping into the activities of a deceased junk dealer.

Then Qwilleran felt a familiar tingling sensation in the roots of his moustache, and he began to argue with himself.

—*But you've got to admit there's something dubious about the setup in Andy's workroom.*

—So he was murdered. So it was a prowler. Attempted robbery.

—*A prowler would whack him on the head and then run. No, the whole incident looked staged. Staged, I said. Did you hear that?*

—If you're thinking about the retired actor, forget it. He's a harmless old codger who likes animals. Koko took to him right away.

—*Don't forget how that avalanche slid off the roof at the appropriate moment. One of those icicles could have brained you. As for Koko, he can be remarkably subjective. He rejected Mrs. Cobb simply because she squeaked at him.*

—Still, it would be interesting to know how she wrenched her back two months ago.

—*Now you're grabbing at straws. She doesn't have the temperament for murder. It takes someone like Mary Duckworth—ice cold, single-minded, extremely capable.*

—You're wrong about her. She can be warm and compassionate. Besides, she would have no motive.

—*Oh, no? She had quarreled with Andy. Who knows how serious it might have been?*

—Undoubtedly they quarreled about the other

woman in his life—still no motive for murder, if she loved him.

—*Perhaps he was threatening to do something that would hurt her more deeply than that.*

—But Mary insists he was kind and thoughtful.

—*He was also dogmatic and intolerant. He might be "doing his duty" again. That kind of person is a classic heel.*

—I wish you'd shut up and let me go to sleep.

Eventually Qwilleran slept, and in the morning he was waked by two hungry cats, playing hopscotch on his bed and miraculously missing his sore knee. Cats had a sixth sense, he noted, that prevented them from hurting the people they liked. He gave them a good breakfast of canned crabmeat.

Later he was applying cold wet towels to his knee when he heard a knock. He took a deep breath of exasperation and moved painfully to open the door.

Iris Cobb was standing there, wearing her hat and coat and holding a plate of coffeecake. "I'm on my way to church," she said. "Would you like some cranberry twists? I got up early and made them. I couldn't sleep."

"Thanks," said Qwilleran, "but I'm afraid you're trying to fatten me up."

"How does the rug look this morning? Did the cream leave a spot?"

"Not bad, but if you want to send it out and have it cleaned, I'll pay for it."

"How's your knee? Any better?"

"These injuries are always worse in the morning. I'm trying cold compresses."

"Why don't you have dinner with us around seven o'clock, and then you won't have to go out of the house. . . . C.C. can tell you some interesting stories about Junktown," she added when Qwilleran hesitated. "We're having pot roast and mashed potatoes—nothing fancy. Just potatoes whipped with sour cream and dill. And a salad with Roquefort dressing. And coconut cake for dessert."

"I'll be there," said Qwilleran.

As soon as he was dressed, he limped to the drugstore, being unable to survive Sunday without the Sunday papers. At the lunch counter he choked down two hard-boiled eggs that were supposed to be soft-boiled and gave himself indigestion by reading Jack Jaunti's new column. Jaunti, who was half Qwilleran's age, now had the gall to write a column of wit and wisdom from the Delphic heights of his adolescent ignorance.

The newsman spent the rest of the day nursing his crippled knee and pecking at his crippled typewriter, and his ailment activated the Florence Nightingale instinct that is common to cats. Every time he sat down, Yum Yum hopped on his lap, while Koko hovered nearby, looked concerned, spoke softly, and purred whenever Qwilleran glanced in his direction.

When seven o'clock arrived, whiffs of beef simmering with garlic and celery tops beckoned the newsman across the hall to the Cobbs' apartment. C.C., shirtless and shoeless, sat with one leg thrown over the arm of his chair and a can of beer in his hand. He grunted at the arriving guest—a welcome more cordial than Qwilleran had expected—and Mrs. Cobb turned joyous eyes on her tenant and ushered him to a stately wing chair.

"It's Charles II," she said. "Best thing we own." She pointed out other treasures, which he admired with reserve: a stuffed owl, a wood carving of an adenoidal eagle, an oil portrait of an infant with a bloated forty-year-old face, and an apothecary desk with two dozen tiny drawers of no use to anyone but an apothecary. A radio on the desk top pounded out a senseless, ceaseless beat.

Mrs. Cobb, playing the fussy hostess, passed a platter of tiny meat turnovers and served small glasses of cranberry juice cocktail on plates with lace paper doilies.

C.C. said, "Who you trying to impress with this fancy grub?"

"Our new tenant, of course. I wouldn't slave over *piroshki* for a slob like you," she said sweetly.

C.C. turned an unshaven but handsome face to Qwilleran. "If she starts buttering you up with her goodies, watch out, mister. She might poison you, like she did her first husband." His tone was belligerent, but Qwilleran caught a glint in the man's eye that was surprisingly affectionate.

"If I poison anybody," his wife said, "it will be Cornball Cobb. . . . Would you all like to hear something interesting?" She reached under a small table and brought a portable tape recorder from its lower shelf. She rewound the reel, touched a green push button and said, "Now listen to this."

As the tape started to unwind, the little machine gave forth an unearthly concert of gurgles, wheezes, whistles, hoots, honks, and snorts.

"Shut that damn thing off!" Cobb yelled, more in sport than in anger.

She laughed. "Now you know how you snore. You wouldn't believe me, would you? You sound like a calliope."

"Did you spend my good money just for that?" He got up and hit the red push button with a fist, silencing the recital, but he wore a peculiar look of satisfaction.

"I'm going to use this for evidence when I sue for divorce." Mrs. Cobb winked at Qwilleran, and he squirmed in his chair. This display of thinly veiled sexuality between husband and wife made him feel like a Peeping Tom.

C.C. said, "When do we eat?"

"He hates my cooking," Iris Cobb said, "but you should see him put it away."

"I can eat anything," her husband grumbled with good humor. "What kind of slop have we got today?"

When they sat down at the big kitchen table, he applied himself to his food and became remarkably genial. Qwilleran tried to visualize C.C. with a shave, a white shirt, and a tie. He could be a successful salesman, a middle-aged matinee idol, a lady-killer, a confidence man. Why had he chosen this grubby role in Junktown?

The newsman ventured to remark, "I met the Three Weird Sisters yesterday," and waited for a reaction.

"How d'you like the redhead?" Cobb asked, leering at his plate. "If she didn't have her foot in a cast, she'd chase you down the street."

"And what do you think of our other tenant?" Mrs. Cobb asked. "Isn't he a funny little man?"

"He puts on a pretty good show," Qwilleran said. "He tells me he was a Broadway actor."

C.C. snorted. "Nearest he ever got to Broadway was Macy's toy department."

His wife said, "Ben loves to play Santa Claus. Every Christmas he puts on a red suit and beard and goes to children's hospital wards."

"They must pay him for it," said C.C. "He wouldn't do it for free."

"One day," she went on, "there was an injured pigeon in the middle of Zwinger Street—with dozens of other pigeons fluttering around to protect it from traffic, and I saw Ben go out with a shoebox and rescue the bird."

Qwilleran said, "He has a repulsive thing in his shop—a stuffed cat on a dusty velvet pillow."

"That's a pincushion. They were all the rage in the Gay Nineties."

"Can he make a living from that dismal collection of junk? Or does he have a sideline, too?"

"Ben's got a bundle salted away," C.C. said. "He

used to make big money in his day—before taxes got so high." Mrs. Cobb gave her husband a startled look.

The man finished eating and pushed his dessert plate away. "I'm gonna scrounge tonight. Anybody want to come?"

"Where do you go?" Qwilleran asked.

"Demolition area. The old Ellsworth house is full of black walnut paneling if I can beat the other vultures to it. Russ says they've already grabbed the stained-glass windows."

"I wish you wouldn't go," his wife said. "It's so cold, and the ice is treacherous, and you know it isn't legal."

"Everybody does it just the same. Where do you think the Dragon got that Russian silver chandelier? She makes like she's so high class, but you should see her with a crowbar!"

Mrs. Cobb said to Qwilleran. "C.C. got caught once and had to pay a heavy fine. You'd think he would have learned his lesson."

"Aw, hell! It won't happen twice," her husband said. "Somebody tipped off the police the other time, and I know who it was. It won't happen again."

"Let's take coffee in the living room," Mrs. Cobb suggested.

Cobb lighted his cigar and Qwilleran lighted his pipe and said, "I understand Junktown doesn't get much cooperation from the city government."

"Mister, you'd think we were some kind of disease that's got to be wiped out," Cobb said. "We asked for better street lights, and the city said no, because Junktown's due to be torn down within the next ten years. *Ten years!* So we tried to put in old-fashioned gaslights at our own expense, but the city said no dice. All light poles gotta be forty feet high."

"C.C. has spent days at City Hall," said Mrs. Cobb, "when he could have been earning good money on the picket line."

"We used to have big elm trees on this street," her husband went on, "and the city cut 'em down to widen the street. So we planted saplings on the curb, and guess what! Chop chop! They widened the street another two feet."

"Tell Qwill about the signs, C.C."

"Yeah, the signs. We all made old-time signs out of wormy wood, and the city made us take 'em down. Unsafe, they said. Then Russ put hand-split cedar shingles on the front of his carriage house, and the city yanked 'em off. Know why? They projected a *half-inch* over the sidewalk! Mister, the city *wants* this neighborhood to decline, so the land-grabbers can get it and the grafters can get their cut!"

"Now we're planning a Christmas Block Party to bring in a little business," said Mrs. Cobb, "but there's so much red tape."

"You gotta get permission to decorate the street. And if you want to play Christmas music outdoors, you get a permit from the Noise Abatement Commission. If you want to give door prizes, you get fingerprinted by the Gambling Commission. If you want to serve refreshments, you get a blood test at the Board of Health. *Nuts!*"

"Maybe the *Daily Fluxion* could expedite matters," Qwilleran suggested. "We have some pull at City Hall."

"Well, I don't care one way or the other. I'm gonna go scrounging."

"I'd go with you," said the newsman, "if I didn't have this bum knee."

Mrs. Cobb said to her husband, "Don't go alone! Can't you get Ben to go with you?"

"That lazy bugger? He wouldn't even carry the flashlight."

"Then ask Mike. He'll go if you give him a couple of dollars." She looked out the window. "It's starting to snow again. I wish you'd stay home."

Without any formal goodbyes, Cobb left the apartment, bundled up in a heavy coat, boots and knitted cap, and after another cup of coffee Qwilleran rose and thanked his hostess for the excellent dinner.

"Do you think the *Fluxion* could do something about our Block Party?" she asked as she accompanied him to the door and gave him a snack for the cats. "It means a lot to C.C. He's like a little boy about Christmas, and I hate to see his heart broken."

"I'll work on it tomorrow."

"Isn't he wonderful when he gets wound up about City Hall?" Her eyes were shining. "I'll never forget the time I went with him to the City Council meeting. He was making things hot for them and the mayor told him to sit down and keep quiet. C.C. said, 'Look buddy, don't tell *me* to pipe down. I pay your salary!' I was so proud of my husband that tears came to my eyes."

Qwilleran went back across the hall, unlocked the door, and peeked in. The cats jumped down from their gilded thrones, knowing that the waxed paper package he carried contained pot roast. Yum Yum rubbed against his ankles, while Koko made loud demands.

The man leaned over to rub Koko's head, and that was when he saw it—on the floor near the desk: a dollar bill! It was folded lengthwise. He knew it was not his own. He never folded his money that way.

"Where did this come from?" he asked the cats. "Has anybody been in here?"

It had to be someone with a key, and he knew it was neither of the Cobbs. He inspected the typed sheets on his desk and the half-finished page in his typewriter. Had someone been curious about what he was writing? It could hardly be anyone but the other tenant in the house. Perhaps Ben doubted that he was a writer—it had happened before—and sneaked in to see for himself, dropping the dollar bill when he pulled something out of his pocket— glasses, or a handkerchief, perhaps. The incident was not really important, but it irritated Qwilleran, and he went back to the Cobb apartment.

"Someone's been snooping around my place," he

told Mrs. Cobb. "Would it be Ben? Does he have a key?"

"Goodness, no! Why would he have a key to your apartment?"

"Well, who else could get in?"

An expression of delight began to spread over the landlady's round face.

"Don't say it! I know!" said Qwilleran with a frown. "She walks through doors."

TWELVE

Early Monday morning, Qwilleran opened his eyes suddenly, not knowing what had waked him. Pain in his knee reminded him where he was—in Junktown, city of sore limbs.

Then the sound that had waked him came again—a knock at the door—not an urgent rapping, not a cheery tattoo, but a slow pounding on the door panel, as ominous as it was strange. Wincing a little, he slid his legs out of bed, put on his robe and answered the summons.

Iris Cobb was standing there, her round face

strained, her eyes swollen. She was wearing a heavy coat and a woolen scarf over her head.

"I'm sorry," she said in a shaken voice. "I've got trouble. C.C. hasn't come home."

"What time is it?"

"Five o'clock. He's never been later than two."

Qwilleran blinked and shook his head and ran his fingers through his hair, as he tried to recall the events of the previous evening. "Do you think the police might have picked him up again?"

"If they had, they'd let him phone me. They did last time."

"What about the boy who was going with him?"

"I've just been around the corner to Mike's house. His mother says he didn't go with C.C. last night. He went to a movie."

"Want me to call the police?"

"No! I don't want them to know he's been scrounging again. I have a feeling he might have fallen and hurt himself."

"Want me to go and see if I can find him?"

"Would you? Oh, would you please? I'll go with you."

"It'll take me a couple of minutes to get dressed."

"I'm sorry to bother you. I'd wake Ben, but he was out drinking half the night."

"That's all right."

"Dress warm. Wear boots." Her voice, normally musical, had flattened out to a gloomy monotone. "I'll call a taxi. C.C. took the station wagon."

"Do you have a flashlight?"

"A small one. C.C. took the big lantern."

As Qwilleran, trying not to limp, took the woman's arm and escorted her down the snow-covered steps to the taxi, he said, "This is going to look peculiar, going to a deserted house at this hour. I'll tell the driver to drop us at the corner. It'll still look odd, but . . ."

The cabdriver said, "Fifteenth and Zwinger? There's nothing there! It's a ghost town."

"We're being met there by another car," Qwilleran said. "My brother—driving in from downriver. A family emergency."

The driver gave an exaggerated shrug and drove them down Zwinger Street. Iris Cobb rode in silence, shivering visibly, and Qwilleran gripped her arm with a steadying hand.

Once she spoke. "I saw something so strange when I was coming home from church yesterday morning. Hundreds of pigeons circling over Junktown—flying round and round and round—a big black cloud. Their wings were like thunder."

At the corner of Fifteenth, Qwilleran gave the driver the folded dollar he had found in his apartment and helped Mrs. Cobb out of the cab. It was a dark night. Other parts of the sky reflected a glow from city lighting, but the street lights in the demolition area were no longer operating.

They waited until the cab was out of sight. Then Qwilleran grasped the woman's arm, and they picked their way across icy ruts where the sidewalk had been cracked by heavy trucks hauling away debris. Several houses had already been leveled, but toward the end of the block stood a large, square, solid house built of stone.

"That's it. That's the one," she said. "It used to have a high iron fence. Some scrounger must have taken it."

There was a carriage entrance at the side. The driveway ran under this porte-cochère, and there was evidence of tire tracks, partially filled with snow. How recent they were, it was impossible to tell.

"I suppose he'd park around back, out of sight," Qwilleran said.

They moved cautiously up the driveway.

"Yes, there's the wagon!" she cried. "He must be here. . . . Can you hear anything?"

They stood still. There was dead silence, except for the lonely whine of tires from the expressway across the open fields.

They went in the back door. "I can hardly walk up the steps," Iris said. "My knees are like jelly. I have a terrible feeling—"

"Take it easy." Qwilleran guided her with a firm hand. "There's a loose board here."

The back door showed signs of having been wrenched open violently. It led into a dust porch and then into a room that had been a large kitchen. Only the upper wall cabinets remained. Lying in the middle of the floor, waiting to be moved out, were a pink marble fireplace and a tarnished brass light fixture.

They paused again and listened. There was no sound. The rooms were dank and icy.

Flashing the light ahead, Qwilleran led the way through a butler's pantry and then a dining room. Gaping holes indicated that the mantel and chandelier had come from this room. Beyond was the parlor, with a large fireplace still intact. A wide archway equipped with sliding doors opened into the front hall, and one of them stood ajar.

Qwilleran went through first, and the woman crowded behind him.

The hall was a shambles. He flashed his light over lengths of stair rail, sections of paneling leaning against the wall, pieces of carved molding, and there—at the foot of the stairs . . .

She screamed. "There he is!" She rushed forward. A large section of paneling lay on top of the sprawled body. "Oh, my God! Is he—Is he—?"

"Maybe he's unconscious. You stay here," Qwilleran said. "Let me have a look."

The slab of black walnut that lay on top of the fallen man was enormously heavy. With difficulty Qwilleran eased it up and tilted it against the wall.

Mrs. Cobb was sobbing. "I'm afraid. Oh, I'm afraid."

Then he beamed the light on the face—white under the gray stubble.

She tugged at Qwilleran's coat. "Can you tell? Is he breathing?"

"It doesn't look good."

"Maybe he's just frozen. Maybe he fell and

knocked himself out, and he's been lying here in the cold." She took her husband's icy hand. She leaned over and flooded warm breath over his nose and mouth.

Neither of them heard the footsteps coming through the house. Suddenly the hall was alight, and the glare of a powerful flashlight blinded them. Someone was standing in the doorway that led from the parlor.

"This is the police," said an official voice behind the light. "What are you doing here?"

Mrs. Cobb burst into tears. "My husband is hurt. Quick! Get him to a hospital."

"What are you doing here?"

"There's no time! No time!" she cried hysterically. "Call an ambulance—call an ambulance before it's too late!"

One of the officers stepped into the beam of light and bent over the body. He shook his head.

"No! No!" she cried wildly. "They can save him! They can do something, I know! Hurry . . . hurry!"

"Too late, lady." Then he said to his partner, "Tell dispatch we've got a body."

Mrs. Cobb uttered a long heartbroken wail.

"You'll have to make a statement at headquarters," the officer said.

Qwilleran showed his police card. "I'm with the *Daily Fluxion*."

The officer nodded and relaxed his brusque manner. "Do you mind coming downtown? The detectives will want a statement. Just routine."

The newsman put an arm around his landlady to support her. "How did you fellows happen to find us?" he asked.

"A cabbie reported two fares dropped at Zwinger and Fifteenth. . . . What happened to this man? Did he fall downstairs?"

"Looks like it. When he failed to come home, we—"

Iris Cobb wailed wretchedly. "He was carrying that panel. He must have slipped—missed his step. . . . I told him not to come. I told him!" She turned a contorted face to Qwilleran. "What will I do? . . . What will I do? . . . I loved that wonderful man!"

THIRTEEN

After Qwilleran had brought Iris Cobb home from Police Headquarters and had called Mary Duckworth to come and stand by, he went to the office. With a bleak expression on his face, accentuated by the downcurve of his moustache, he threw ten pages of triple-spaced copy on Arch Riker's desk.

"What's the matter?" Arch said.

"Rough morning! I've been up since five," Qwilleran told him. "My landlord was killed. Fell down a flight of stairs."

"You mean Cobb?"

"He was stripping one of the condemned houses, and when he didn't come home, I went out with Mrs. Cobb to look for him. We found him dead at the foot of the stairs. Then the police took us in for questioning. Mrs. Cobb is a wreck."

"Too bad. Sorry to hear that."

"It was the Ellsworth house on Fifteenth Street."

"I know the place," Riker said. "A big stone mausoleum. Hector Ellsworth was mayor of this town forty years ago."

"He was?" Qwilleran laughed without mirth. "Then Cobb lost his last battle with City Hall. They finally got him! I'm beginning to believe in the spirit world."

"How are you going to write this up?"

"It's a trifle awkward. Cobb was trespassing."

"Scrounging? All the junkers do that. Even Rosie! She never goes out without a crowbar in the car."

"Tell your wife she's guilty of looting city property. Cobb was caught once. They arrested him and gave him a heavy fine—and a warning, which he disregarded."

"Doesn't sound like the kind of jolly Christmas story the boss wants."

"There's one thing we could do," said Qwilleran. "Cobb was organizing a Christmas celebration for Junktown—a Block Party— and the city was giving him a hard time. Wouldn't let him decorate the street, play Christmas music, or serve refreshments. All kinds of red tape. Why don't we talk to City Hall and railroad this thing through for Wednesday afternoon? It's the least we can do. It's not much, but it might make the widow feel a little better."

"I'll ask the boss to get the mayor on the phone."

"The way I see it, there are five city bureaus giving Junktown the run-around. If they could just get someone from the mayor's office to cut through the whole mess . . . "

"All right. And why don't you write a plug for the Block Party? We'll run it in tomorrow's paper. We'll get every junker in town to turn out. And write something about Cobb—something with heart."

Qwilleran nodded. The phrases were already forming in his mind. He'd write about the man who tried to make people hate him, but in the topsy-turvy world of the junker, everyone loved his perversity.

Qwilleran stopped in the *Fluxion* library to look up the clips on Hector Ellsworth and at the payroll cage to pick up his check, and then he returned to Junktown.

Mary Duckworth, handsomely trousered, met him at the door of the Cobb apartment. He was aware of a subtle elation in her manner.

"How's Iris?" he asked.

"I gave her a sedative, and she's sleeping. The funeral will be in Cleveland, and I've made a plane reservation for her."

"Anything I can do? Perhaps I should pick up the station wagon. It's still behind the Ellsworth house. Then I can drive her to the airport."

"Would you? I'm packing a bag for her."

"When she wakes," Qwilleran said, "tell her that Junktown is going to have everything C.C. wanted for the Christmas party."

"I know," said Mary. "The mayor's office has already called. His representative is coming here to speak to the dealers this afternoon, and then we'll have a meeting upstairs tonight."

"In Hernia Heaven? I'd like to attend."

"The dealers would be delighted to have you."

"Come across the hall," Qwilleran said. "I have something to report."

As he unlocked the door of his apartment, the cats—who had been curled together in a sleeping pillow of fur in the Morris chair—immediately raised their heads. Yum Yum scampered from the room, but Koko stood his ground, arching his back and bushing his tail as he glared at the stranger. His reaction was not hostile—only unflattering.

"Do I look like an ogre?" Mary wanted to know.

"Koko can sense Hepplewhite," Qwilleran said. "He knows you've got a big dog. Cats are psychic."

He threw his overcoat on the daybed and placed his hat on the desk, and when he did so, he saw a small dark object lying near his typewriter. He approached it gingerly. It looked like the decomposed remains of a small bird.

"What's this?" he said. "What the devil is this?"

Mary examined the small brown fragment. "Why, it's a piece of hair jewelry! A brooch!"

He combed his moustache with his fingertips. "Some uncanny things have been happening on

these premises. Yesterday some benevolent spirit left
me a dollar bill!" He examined the birdlike form
woven of twisted brown strands. "You mean this is
real hair?"

"Human hair. It's memorial jewelry. They used to
make necklaces, bracelets, all sorts of things from
the hair of someone who had died."

"Who would want to keep such stuff?"

"Iris has an extensive collection. She even wears it
occasionally."

Qwilleran dropped the brooch with distaste. "Sit
down," he said, "and let me tell you what I discovered about the Ellsworth house in the *Fluxion* clip
file." He offered her a gilded chair, flipping the red
cushion to the side that was not furred with cat hair.
"Did you know that Ellsworth was a former
mayor?"

"Yes, I've heard about him."

"He died at the age of ninety-two, having
achieved a reputation for eccentricity. He was a
compulsive collector—never threw anything away.
He had a twenty-year accumulation of old newspapers, string, and vinegar bottles. And he was supposed to be worth quite a sum of money, but a large
chunk of his holdings was never found. . . . Does
that suggest anything to you?"

Mary shook her head.

"Suppose someone was looking for buried treasure in the old house last night . . . and suppose C.C.
arrived with his crowbar, looking for black walnut

paneling . . . and suppose they thought he was after the strongbox?"

"Don't you think that's rather far-fetched?"

"Maybe he accidentally found the loot when he ripped open the paneling . . . and maybe another scrounger came along and pushed him downstairs. I admit it's far-fetched, but it's a possibility."

The girl looked at Qwilleran with sudden curiosity. "Is it true what my father says about you? That you've solved two murder cases since joining the *Fluxion*?"

"Well, I was instrumental—that is, I didn't do it alone. I had help." He touched his moustache tentatively and threw a glance in Koko's direction. Koko was watching, and he was all ears.

"Do you really think that Cobb might have been murdered?"

"Murder shouldn't be ruled out too quickly—although the police accepted it as an accident. A man with Cobb's personality must have had enemies."

"His churlishness was a pose—for business reasons. Everyone knew that. Many junkers think prices go up if a dealer is friendly, and if his shop is clean."

"Whether it was an act or not, I don't suppose anyone hated him enough to kill him. Competition for the Ellsworth treasure would make a better motive."

Mary stood up and looked out the back window for a while. "I don't know whether this will have any bearing on the case," she said finally, "but . . . when C.C. went scrounging late at night, he didn't always go to a condemned building."

"You think he was playing around?"

"I know he was."

"Anybody we know?"

Mary hesitated and then said, "One of The Three Weird Sisters."

Qwilleran gave a dry chuckle. "I can guess which one."

"She's a nymphomaniac," said Mary with her cool porcelain look.

"Did Iris suspect?"

"I don't think so. She's near-sighted in more ways than one."

"How did you know this was going on?"

"Mrs. Katzenhide lives in the same apartment building. Several times she saw Cobb paying late evening calls, and you know very well he was not there to discuss the hallmarks on English silver."

Qwilleran studied Mary's face. Her eyes were sparkling, and her personality had a new buoyancy.

"What's happened to you, Mary?" he asked. "You've changed."

She smiled joyously. "I feel as if I've been living under a cloud, and the sun has just broken through!"

"Can you tell me about it?"

"Not now. Later. I'd better go back to Iris. She'll wake and think she's deserted."

After she had left, Qwilleran took another look at the hair brooch—and a good hard look at the cats.

The male was graciously allowing the female to wash his ears.

"Okay, Koko, the game's up," he said. "Where are you getting this loot?"

Koko sat very tall and squeezed his eyes innocently.

"You feline Fagin! I'll bet you find the stuff, and you make Yum Yum steal it. Where's your secret cache?"

Koko unfolded his rear half and with dignity walked from the room. Qwilleran followed him—into the bathroom.

"You're finding them under the tub?"

"Yow," said Koko with a noncommittal inflection.

Qwilleran started to go down on all fours, but a twinge in his bad knee discouraged the effort. "I'll bet no one's cleaned under that monster for fifty years," he told the cat, who was now sitting in his sandbox with a soulful look in his eyes and paying no attention to anyone.

Shortly after, when Qwilleran returned to the Ellsworth house to pick up the Cobb car, he did some treasure hunting of his own. He looked for footprints and tire tracks in the snow and telltale marks in the dust of the stripped rooms.

White plaster dust had settled everywhere. Large objects had been dragged through it, leaving dark trails, and footprints had piled on footprints, but here and there a mark could be distinguished. Qwilleran noticed the patterned treads of boots, the imprint of a claw hammer, some regularly spaced dots (made by crutches?), and even the pawprints of a large animal, and a series of feathery arabesques in the dust, perhaps caused by the switching of a tail. Evidently ever dealer in Junktown had been through the Ellsworth house at one time or another; recent prints were lightly filmed over and the older ones were almost covered.

Qwilleran dug Cobb's flashlight out of a pile of rubble and retrieved his crowbar. Then he went upstairs. Everything on the stair treads had been obliterated, but on the landing there was evidence of three kinds of footwear, and although it was impossible to guess whether all three had been there at the same time, they were sharp enough to be recent.

The newsman copied the tread marks on the folded sheet of newsprint that was always in his pocket. One print was a network of diamond shapes, another was a series of closely spaced dots, and the third was crossbarred. His own galoshes left a pattern of small circles.

The tire tracks in the yard contributed nothing to Qwilleran's investigation. There was no telling how many junkers had been in and out of the driveway. Tire tracks had crisscrossed and frozen and melted and frozen again, and snow had frosted the unreadable hieroglyphics.

Qwilleran backed the tan station wagon out of its hiding place in the backyard, and as he pulled away, he noticed that the vehicle left a rectangle of gray in the field of white snow. He also noticed another such rectangle nearby. Two cars had parked there on the dirty ice Sunday night, after which a light snow had fallen. Qwilleran jumped out of the wagon, thanked fate and Mary Duckworth for the tape line in his pocket, and measured the length and breadth of the second rectangle. It was shorter than the imprint left by the Cobb wagon, and it was not quite square at one corner, the snow having drifted in from the northwest.

Qwilleran's findings did not amount to much, he had to admit. Even if the owner of the second car were known, there was no proof that he had engineered Cobb's fatal fall. Nevertheless, the mere routine of investigation was exhilarating to Qwilleran, and he drove from the scene with a feeling of accomplishment. On second impulse he drove back into the Ellsworth yard, entered the house, and salvaged two items for the Cobb Junkery: a marble mantel and a chandelier of blackened brass.

Later he drove Mrs. Cobb to the airport.

"I don't have anything black to wear," she said wearily. "C.C. always liked me to wear bright colors. Pink especially." She huddled on the car seat in her cheap coat with imitation fur lining, her pink crocheted church-going hat, and her two pairs of glasses hanging from ribbons."

"You can pick up something in Cleveland," Qwilleran said, "if you think it's necessary. Who's going to meet you there?"

"My brother-in-law—and Dennis, if he gets in from St. Louis."

"Is that your son?"

"Yes."

"What's he doing in St. Louis?"

"He finished school last June and just started his first job."

"Does he like antiques?"

"Oh, dear, no! He's an architect!"

Keep her talking, Qwilleran thought. "How old is he?"

"Twenty-two."

"Single?"

"Engaged She's a nice girl. I wanted to give them some antique silver for Christmas, but Dennis doesn't approve of anything old. . . . Oh, dear! I forgot the presents for the mailman and the milkman. There are two envelopes behind the clock in the kitchen—with a card and a little money in them. Will you see that they get them—in case I don't come home right away? I wrapped up a little Christmas treat for Koko and Yum Yum, too. It's in the top drawer of the Empire chest. And tell Ben that I'll make his bourbon cake when I get back from the— from Cleveland."

"How do you make bourbon cake?" Keep her talking.

"With eggs and flour and walnuts and raisins and a cup of bourbon."

"Nothing could beat that coconut cake you made yesterday."

"Coconut was C.C.'s favorite," she said, and then she fell silent, staring straight ahead but seeing nothing beyond the windshield.

FOURTEEN

When Qwilleran returned from the airport in the Cobb station wagon, he saw a fifth of a ton of *Flux ion* photographer squeezing into a Volkswagen at the curb.

"Tiny!" he hailed him. "Did you get everything?"

"I went to five places," Tiny said. "Shot six rolls."

"I've got another idea. Do you have a wide angle lens? How about shooting a picture of my apartment? To show how people live in Junktown."

The staircase groaned when the photographer followed Qwilleran upstairs, and Yum Yum gave one look at the outsize stranger decked with strange apparatus and promptly took flight. Koko observed the proceedings with aplomb.

Tiny cast a bilious glance around the room. "How can you live with these crazy anachronisms?"

"They grow on you," Qwilleran said smugly.

"Is that a bed? Looks like a funeral barge on the Nile. And who's your embalmed friend over the fireplace? You know, these junk dealers are a bunch of graverobbers. One guy wanted me to photograph a dead cat, and those three dames with all that rusty tin were swooning over some burial jewelry from an Inca tomb."

"You're not tuned in," Qwilleran said with the casual air of authority that comes easily to a newsman after three days on a new beat. "Antiques have character—a sense of history. See this bookrack? You wonder where it's been—who owned it—what books it's held—who polished the brass. An English butler? A Massachusetts poet? An Ohio schoolteacher?"

"You're a bunch of necrophiles," said Tiny. "My God! Even the cat!" He stared at Yum Yum, trudging into the room with a small dead mouse.

"Drop that dirty thing!" Qwilleran shouted, stamping his foot.

She dropped it and streaked out of sight. He scooped up the gray morsel on a sheet of paper, rushed it into the bathroom and flushed it down the toilet.

After Tiny had left, Qwilleran sat at his typewriter, aware of an uncommon silence in the house. The cats were snoozing, the Cobb radio was quiet, Ben was about his business elsewhere, and The Junkery was closed. When the doorbell rang, it startled him.

There was a man waiting on the stoop—an ordinary-looking man in an ordinary-looking gray car coat.

"Sorry to bother you," he said. "I'm Hollis Prantz. I have a shop down the street. Just heard the bad news about brother Cobb."

Qwilleran nodded with the appropriate amount of gloom.

"Rotten time of year to have it happen," said Prantz. "I hear Mrs. Cobb has left town."

"She went to Cleveland for the funeral."

"Well, tell you why I came. Cobb was saving some old radios for me, and I could probably unload them in my shop during the shindig tomorrow. Mrs. Cobb would appreciate it, I'm sure. Every little bit helps at a time like this."

Qwilleran waved toward The Junkery. "Want to go in and have a look?"

"Oh, they wouldn't be in their shop. Cobb had put them aside in his apartment, he said."

The newsman took time to pat his moustache before saying, "Okay, go on upstairs," and he added, "I'll help you look."

"Don't trouble yourself. I'll find them." The dealer bounded up the stairs, two at a time.

"No trouble," Qwilleran insisted, following as

quickly as he could and trying to catch a glimpse of the man's boot soles. He stayed close behind as Prantz opened a coat closet, the window seat, the armoire.

"Look, friend, I hate to take up your time. I know you must be busy. You're writing that series for the paper, they tell me."

"No problem," said Qwilleran. "Glad to stretch my legs." He watched the dealer's eyes as they roved around the apartment and returned repeatedly to the desk—the apothecary desk with its tall bank of miniature drawers. Crowded on top of the lofty superstructure were some pewter candlesticks, the stuffed owl, a tin box, a handful of envelopes, and the Cobbs' overworked radio.

"What I'm interested in," said Prantz, "is equipment from the early days—crystal sets and old beehive radios. Not so easy to come by. . . . Well, sorry to trouble you."

"I'll be in to see your shop," Qwilleran said, ushering him out of the apartment.

"Sure! It's a little unusual, and you might get a bang out of it."

The newsman looked at the dealer's footwear. "Say, did you buy those boots around here? I need a pair like that."

"No, these are old," said Prantz. "I don't even remember where I bought them, but they're just ordinary boots."

"Do the soles have a good grip?"

"Good enough, although the treads are beginning to wear slick."

The dealer left without offering Qwilleran a view of his soles, and the newsman telephoned Mary Duckworth at once. "What do you know about Hollis Prantz?" he asked.

"Not much. He's new on the street. He sells techtiques, whatever they may be."

"I noticed his shop the first day I was here. Looks like a TV repair shop."

"He has some preposterous theories."

"About what?"

"About 'artificially accelerated antiquity.' Frankly, I haven't decided whether he's a prophetic genius or a psychopath."

"Has he been friendly with the Cobbs?"

"He tries to be friendly with everyone. Really *too* friendly. Why are you interested?"

"Prantz was just over here. Invited me to see his shop," the newsman said. "By the way, have you ever been to the Ellsworth house?"

"No, I haven't, but I know which one it is. The Italianate sandstone on Fifteenth Street."

"When you go scrounging, do you ever take Hepplewhite?"

"Scrounging! I never go scrounging! I handle nothing but eighteenth century English."

After his conversation with Mary, Qwilleran looked for Koko. "Come on, old boy," he said to the room at large. "I've got an assignment for you."

There was no response from Koko, but Yum Yum

was staring at the third shelf of the book cupboard, and that meant he was snuggling behind the biographies. That's where Qwilleran had first met Koko— on a shelf between the lives of Van Gogh and Leonardo da Vinci.

He pulled the cat out and showed him a tangle of blue leather straps and white cord. "Do you know what this is?"

Koko had not worn the harness since the day in early autumn when he had saved Qwilleran's life. On that occasion he had performed some sleight-of-paw with the four yards of nylon cord that served as a leash. Now he allowed the halter to be slipped over his head and the belt to be buckled under his soft white underside. His body pulsed with a rasping purr of anticipation.

"We'll leave Yum Yum here to mind the house," Qwilleran told him, "and we'll go and play bloodhound."

As soon as the apartment door was opened, Koko bounded like a rabbit toward the furniture stacked at the front end of the hall, and before Qwilleran could haul in the cord, the cat had squeezed between the spindles of a chair, scuttled under a chest of drawers, circled the leg of a spinning wheel, and effectively tangled the leash, leaving himself free to sniff the finial hidden in the jumble.

"You think you're smart, don't you?" Qwilleran said, as he worked to free the cord and extricate the cat. Some minutes later, he lugged the protesting Koko, squirming and squawking, to the door of the

Cobb apartment. "I have news for you. This is where we're going to explore."

Koko sniffed the corner of the worn Oriental rug before setting foot on it. Then, to Qwilleran's delight he walked directly to the apothecary desk, stopping only to scratch his back on a copper coal-hod filled with magazines. At the desk Koko hopped to the chair seat and then to the writing surface, where he moved his nose from right to left across an envelope that had come in the mail.

"Find anything interesting?" Qwilleran inquired, but it was only a telephone bill.

Next Koko reared on his haunches and regarded the bank of small drawers—twenty-four of them with white porcelain knobs—and selected one on which to rub his jaw. His white fangs clicked on the white ceramic, and Qwilleran gingerly opened the drawer he indicated. It contained a set of false teeth made of wood. Guiltily the newsman opened other drawers and found battered silver spoons, primitive eyeglasses, tarnished jewelry, and a few bracelets made of hair. Most of the drawers were empty.

While Qwilleran was thus occupied, a feather floated past his nose. Koko had stealthily risen to the top of the drawer deck and was nuzzling the stuffed owl.

"I might have known!" Qwilleran said in disgust. "Get down! Get away from that bird!

Koko sailed to the floor and stalked haughtily from the apartment, leading the newsman behind him on a slack leash.

"I'm disappointed in you," the man told him. "You used to be good at this sort of thing. Let's try the attic."

The attic room had been romantically remodeled to resemble a barn, the walls paneled with silvery weathered planks and hung with milking stools, oil lanterns, and old farm implements. A papier-mâché steer, relic of a nineteenth century butcher shop, glared out of a corner stall, and a white leghorn brooded on a nest of straw.

In the center of the room, chairs were arranged in a circle, and Qwilleran was fascinated by their decrepitude. He noted an ice cream parlor chair of wire construction, badly bent; a Windsor with two spindles missing; a porch rocker with one arm, and other seating pieces in various stages of collapse. While he was viewing these derelicts, Koko was stalking the white feathered biddy on her nest.

The man yanked the leash. "I don't know what's happened to you," he said. "Pigeons—owls—hens! I think I'm feeding you too much poultry. Come on. Let's go."

Koko rushed downstairs and clamored to get into his apartment, where Yum Yum was calling him with high, pitched mews.

"Oh, no, you don't! We have one more investigation to make. And this time try to be objective."

In Ben's apartment furniture was herded together without plan, and every surface was piled high with items of little worth. Ben's long knitted muffler was draped incongruously over the chandelier, dangling its soiled tassels, and his many hats—including the silk topper and the Santa Claus cap—were to be seen on tables, hatracks, chair seats and lamp chimneys.

Qwilleran found the apartment layout similar to his own, with the addition of a large bay window in the front. With one ear tuned to the sound of a downstairs door opening, he stepped cautiously into each room, finding dirty dishes in the kitchen sink and a ring in the bathtub, as he had expected. In the dressing room, jammed to the ceiling with bundles and boxes, he looked for boots, but Ben, wherever he was, had them on his feet.

"No clues here," Qwilleran said, starting toward the door and casually lifting his red feather from Ben's silk topper. He yanked the leash. "And you're no help any more. It was a mistake to get you a companion. You've lost your talent."

He had not noticed Koko, sitting up like a squirrel, batting the tassels of Ben's long scarf.

FIFTEEN

When the time came for the meeting in Hernia Heaven, Qwilleran climbed to the third floor with some discomfort. His bad knee, although it had improved during the day, tightened up at nightfall, and he arrived at the meeting with a noticeable limp.

The dealers sat in a circle, and Qwilleran looked at their feet before he looked at their faces. They had tramped upstairs in their outdoor togs, and he saw velvet boots, a single brown suede teamed with a walking cast, some man-sized boots in immaculate white, and assorted rubbers and galoshes.

He took the nearest vacant seat—on a church pew

with threadbare cushions—and found himself sitting between Cluthra's cast and Russ Patch's crutches.

"Looks like the bus stop for Lourdes," said the redhead with a fraternal lean in Qwilleran's direction. "What happened to you?"

"I was felled by an avalanche."

"I wouldn't have struggled up all those stairs, one sloggin' foot at a time, only I heard you were going to be here." She gave him a wink and a friendly nudge.

"How did the picture-taking go?" he asked.

"That photographer you sent is a big hunk of man."

"Did he break anything?"

"Only a small Toby jug."

"Newspapers always assign bulls to china shops," Qwilleran explained. He was trying to see the soles of the footwear around him, but every pair of feet remained firmly planted on the floor. He turned to Russell Patch and said, "Good-looking boots you're wearing. Where did you manage to find white ones?"

"Had to have them custom-made," said the young man, stretching out his good leg for advantageous display.

"Even the soles are white!" Qwilleran said, staring at the ridged bottoms and patting his moustache with satisfaction. "I suppose those crutches cramp your style when it comes to scrounging."

"I still get around, and I won't have to use them much longer."

"Get anything out of the Ellsworth house?"

"No, I skipped that one. The kitchen cabinets were grabbed off before I could get there, and that's all I'm interested in."

They lie, Qwilleran thought. All these dealers lie. They're all actors, unable to tell reality from fantasy. Aloud he said, "What do you do with kitchen cabinets?"

"The real old ones make good built-ins for stereo installations, if you give them a provincial finish. I've got a whole wall of them myself, with about twenty thousand dollars worth of electronic equipment. Thirty-six speakers. You like music? I've got everything on tape. Operas, symphonies, chamber music, classic jazz—"

"You must have quite an investment there," Qwilleran said, alerted to the apparent wealth of this young man.

"Priceless! Come up and have a listen some night. I live right over my shop, you know."

"Do you own the building?"

"Well, it's like this. I rented it for a while and built in so many improvements—me and my roommate, that is—that I had to buy it to protect my investment."

Qwilleran forgot to pry any further, because Mary Duckworth arrived. Wearing a short blue plaid skirt, she sat on a kitchen chair of the Warren Harding period and crossed her long elegant legs. For the first time Qwilleran saw her knees. He considered himself a connoisseur of knees, and these had all the correct points. They were slender, shapely, and eminently designed for their function—with the kind of vertical indentations on either side of the kneecap that caused a stir in the roots of his moustache.

"My Gawd! *She's* here!" said a husky voice in his ear. "Keep her away from me, will you? She might try to break the other one." The redhead's ample bosom heaved with anger. "You know, she deliberately dropped a cast-iron garden urn on my foot."

"Mary did?"

"*That woman,*" she said between clenched teeth, "is capable of *anything!* I wish she'd get out of Junktown! Her shop doesn't belong here. That high-priced pedigreed stuff spoils it for the rest of us."

There was a sudden round of applause as Ben Nicholas, who had been acting as doorman down below, made a grandiose entrance in an admiral's cocked hat, and then the meeting began.

Sylvia Katzenhide reviewed the plans for the Block Party on Wednesday. "The city is going to rope off four blocks," she said, "and decorate the utility poles with plastic angels. They've run out of Christmas angels, but they have some nice lavender ones left over from last Easter. Carol singers will be supplied by the Sanitation Department Glee Club."

Qwilleran said, "Could we keep The Junkery open during the party? I hate to see Mrs. Cobb lose that extra business. I'd be willing to mind the store for a couple of hours myself."

Cluthra squeezed his arm and said, "You're a

honey! We'll help, too—my sisters and I. We'll take turns."

Then someone suggested sending flowers to the Cobb funeral, and just as they were taking up a collection, they were stunned by a blast of noise from the floor below. It was a torrent of popular music—raucous, bouncy, loud. They listened in open-mouthed astonishment for a few seconds, then all talked at once.

"What's that?"

"A radio?"

"Who's down there?"

"Nobody!"

"Where's it coming from?"

"Somebody's downstairs!"

"Who could it be?"

"How could they get in?"

"The front door's locked, isn't it?"

Qwilleran was the first one on his feet. "Let's go down and see." He grabbed a wooden sledge hammer that was hanging on the wall and started down the narrow stairs, left foot first on each step. The only other men at the meeting followed—Russ on his crutches and Ben lumbering after them with a pitchfork in his hand.

The noise was coming from the Cobb apartment. The door stood open. The apartment was in darkness.

Qwilleran reached in, groped for a wall switch and flooded the room with light. "Who's there?" he shouted in a voice of authority.

There was no answer. The music poured out of the small radio on the apothecary desk.

The three men searched the apartment, Ben bringing up a delayed rear.

"No one here," Qwilleran announced.

"Maybe it has an automatic timer," Russ said.

"The thing doesn't have a timer," Qwilleran said as he turned off the offensive little radio. He frowned at the writing surface of the desk. Papers were scattered. A pencil cup was knocked over. From the floor he picked up a telephone bill and an address book—and a gray feather.

As the men emerged from the Cobb apartment, the women were beginning to venture down from the attic.

"Is it safe?" they asked.

Cluthra said, "If it was a man, which way did he go?"

"What was it? Does anyone know what it was?"

"That crazy radio," Russ said. "It turned on all by itself."

"How could it do that?"

"I don't know," said Qwilleran . . . but he did.

After the dealers had straggled out the front door and Ben had departed for an evening at The Lion's Tail, Qwilleran unlocked his apartment door and looked for the cats. Yum Yum was sitting on top of the refrigerator with eyes bright and ears alert—eyes and ears a trifle too large for her tiny wedge-shaped face. Koko was lapping up a drink of water, his tail lying straight on the floor as it did when he was especially thirsty.

"Okay, Koko," said Qwilleran. "How did you do it? Have you teamed up with Mathilda?"

The tip of Koko's tail tapped the floor lightly, as he went on drinking.

Qwilleran wandered through his suite of rooms and speculated on each one. He knew Koko could turn a radio dial by scraping it with his hard little jaw, but how was this feline Houdini getting out of the apartment? Qwilleran moved the swan bed away from the wall and looked for a vent in the baseboard. He examined the bathroom for trap doors (turn-of-the-century plumbers had been fond of trap doors), but there was nothing of the sort. The kitchenette had a high transom window cut through to the hall, presumably for ventilation, and it would be easily accessible from the top of the refrigerator, but it was closed and latched.

The telephone rang.

"Qwill," said Mary's pleasing voice, "are you doing anything about your knee? You looked as if you were in pain tonight."

"I used cold compresses until the swelling went down."

"What you need now is a heat lamp. May I offer you mine?"

"I'd appreciate it," he said. "Yes, I'd appreciate it very much."

In preparation for his session with the heat lamp, Qwilleran put on a pair of sporty walking shorts that had survived a country weekend the previous summer and admired himself in the long mirror on the dressing room door, at the same time pulling in his waistline and expanding his chest. He had always thought he would look admirable in Scottish kilts. His legs were straight, solid, muscular and moderately haired—just enough to look virile, not enough to look zoological. The puffiness around the left knee that had destroyed its perfection had now subsided, he was glad to note.

He told the cats, "I'm having a guest, and I want you guys to use some discretion. No noisy squabbles! No flying around and disturbing the status quo!"

Koko squeezed his eyes and tilted his whiskers in what looked like a knowing smile. Yum Yum exhibited indifference by laundering the snow-white cowlick where her fur grew in two directions on her breast.

When Mary arrived, carrying a basket, Koko looked her over from an unfriendly distance.

"He's not overwhelmed with joy," she said, "but at least he's civil this time."

"He'll get used to you," Qwilleran assured her.

In her basket she had homemade fruitcake and an espresso maker, as well as a heat lamp. She plugged in the little silver coffee machine and positioned the infrared lamp over Qwilleran's knee and then sat in the twiggy rocker. Immediately the country bumpkin of a rocking chair looked gracefully linear and organically elegant, and Qwilleran wondered why he had ever thought it was ugly.

"Do you have any idea what caused the outburst in the Cobb apartment?" she asked.

"Just another of the cockeyed things that happen in this house. . . . By the way, I wonder why Hollis Prantz didn't attend the meeting."

"Half the dealers stayed away. They probably knew we'd collect money for flowers."

"Prantz was here this afternoon, looking for some antique radios the Cobbs were supposed to be saving for him—or so he said. Does that make sense?"

"Oh, certainly. Dealers make most of their money by selling to each other. . . . How does the heat feel? Is the lamp too close?"

Soon a rushing, bubbling roar in the kitchen announced that the espresso was ready. It alarmed Yum Yum, who ran in the opposite direction, but Koko made it his business to march into the kitchen and investigate.

With a mixture of pride and apology Qwilleran said, "Koko's a self-assured fellow, but Yum Yum's as nervous as a cat; when in doubt, she exits. She's what you might call a pussycat's pussycat. She sits on laps and catches mice—all the things cats are supposed to do."

"I've never owned a cat," Mary said as she poured the coffee in small cups and added a twist of lemon peel. "But I used to study them for their grace of movement when I was dancing."

"No one ever owns a cat," he corrected her. "You

share a common habitation on a basis of equal rights and mutual respect . . . although somehow the cat always comes out ahead of the deal. Siamese particularly have a way of getting the upper hand."

"Some animals are almost human. . . . Please try this fruitcake, Qwill."

He accepted a dark, moist, mysterious, aromatic wedge of cake. "Koko is more than human. He has a sixth sense. He seems to have access to information that a human couldn't collect without laborious investigation." Qwilleran heard himself saying it, and he hoped it was still true, but deep in his heart he was beginning to wonder.

Mary turned to look at the remarkable animal. Koko was sitting on his spine with one leg in midair as he washed the base of his tail. He paused with pink tongue extended and returned her admiring gaze with an insolent stare. Then, having finished his ablutions, he went on to the ritual of sharpening his claws. He jumped on the daybed, stood on his hind legs and scratched the papered wall where the book pages overlapped and corners were beginning to curl up tantalizingly.

"No! Down! Scram! Beat it!" Qwilleran scolded. Koko obeyed, but not until he had finished the sharpening job and taken his time about it.

The man explained to his guest. "Koko was given a dictionary for a scratching pad, and now he thinks he can use any printed page for a pedicure. Sometimes I'm convinced he can read. He once exposed a series of art forgeries that way."

"Are you serious?"

"Absolutely. . . . Tell me, is there much fakery in antiques?"

"Not in this country. An unscrupulous dealer may sell a nineteenth century Chippendale reproduction as an eighteenth century piece, or an artist may do crude paintings on old canvas and call them early American primitives, but there's no large-scale faking to my knowledge. . . . How do you like the fruitcake? One of my customers made it. Robert Maus."

"The attorney?"

"Do you know him? He's a superb cook."

"Wasn't he Andy's lawyer? Quite an important attorney for a little operation in Junktown," Qwilleran remarked.

"Robert is an avid collector and a friend of mine. He represented Andy as a courtesy."

"Did his legal mind ever do any questioning about Andy's so-called accident?"

Mary gave him an anxious glance. "Are you still pursuing that?"

Qwilleran decided to be candid. He was tired of hearing about Andy's superlative qualities from all the women in Junktown. "Are you aware," he said, "that it was Andy who tipped off the police to Cobb's scrounging?"

"No, I can't believe—"

"Why did he squeal on Cobb and not on Russ or some of the other scroungers? Did he have a grudge against Cobb?"

"I don't—"

"It may be that Andy also threatened Cobb— threatened to tell Iris about his philandering. I hate to say this, Mary, but your friend Andy was a meddler—or else he had an ax to grind. Perhaps he considered that Cobb was trespassing on his own territory when he visited Cluthra."

Mary flushed. "So you found out about *that*, too!"

"I'm sorry," said Qwilleran. "I didn't want to embarrass you."

She shrugged, and she was attractive when she shrugged. "I knew that Andy was seeing Cluthra. That's why we quarreled the night he was killed. Andy and I weren't really committed. We had an understanding. Not even an understanding—just an arrangement. But I'm afraid I was beginning to feel possessive." She reached over and clicked off the heat lamp. "That knee has broiled long enough. How does it feel?"

"Better. Much better." Qwilleran started to fill his pipe. "After Andy left your house that night—to meet the prospective customers—what route did he take?"

"He went out my back door, through the alley and into the back of his shop."

"And when you followed, you went the same way? Did you see anyone else in the alley?"

Mary gave Qwilleran a swift glance. "I don't think so. There might have been one of those invisible men from the rooming house. They slink around like ghosts."

"How much time had elapsed when you followed Andy?"

She hesitated. "Oh . . . about an hour . . . More fruitcake, Qwill?"

"Thanks. During that time the customers may have come, found the front door locked, and gone away—unaware that Andy lay dead in the back room. Before they arrived, someone else could have followed Andy into his shop through the back door—someone who had seen him enter. . . . Let's see, how many buildings stand between your house and Andy's store?"

"Russ's carriage house, then the variety store, then this house, then the rooming house where Ben has his shop."

"That building and your own place are duplicates of this house, aren't they?" Qwilleran asked. "Only narrower."

"You're very observant. The three houses were built by the same family."

"I know Russ lives upstairs over his workshop. Who's his roommate? Is he in the antique business?"

"No. Stanley is a hairdresser."

"I wonder where Russ gets all his dough. He owns the carriage house, wears custom-made boots, has twenty thousand dollars worth of sound equipment, stables a white Jaguar. . . . Is he on the up-and-up? Did Andy think he was simon-pure? Maybe Andy was getting ready to put the finger on him. Where *does* Russ get his dough? Does he have a sideline?"

"I only know that he's a hard worker. Sometimes I hear his power tools at three o'clock in the morning."

"I wonder—" Qwilleran stopped to light his pipe. "I wonder why Russ lied to me tonight. I asked him if he'd been scrounging at the Ellsworth house, and he denied it. Yet I could swear that those crutches and those white boots had been through that house."

"Dealers are sensitive about their sources of supply," Mary said. "It's considered bad form to ask a dealer where he acquires his antiques, and if he answers you at all, he never feels bound to state the truth. It's also bad form to tell a dealer about your grandmother's attic treasures."

"Really? Who decrees these niceties of etiquette?"

Mary smiled in a lofty way that Qwilleran found charming. "The same authority who gives newspapers the right to invade everyone's privacy."

"Touché!"

"Did I tell you about finding the twenty dollar bill?" she asked after they had gazed at each other appreciatively for a few seconds.

"Some people get all the breaks," he said. "Where did you find it?"

"In the pocket of my sweater—the one I was wearing on the night of Andy's accident. The sweater dipped in his blood, and I rolled it up in a ball and stuffed it on a closet shelf. My cleaning woman found it this weekend, and that's when the twenty dollar bill came to light."

"Where did it come from?"

"I picked it up in Andy's workroom."

"You mean you found money at the scene of the accident? And you picked it up? Didn't you realize it might be an important clue?"

Mary shrugged and looked appealingly guilty. "Banker's child," she explained.

"Was it folded?"

She nodded.

"How was it folded?"

"Lengthwise—and then in half."

"Did Andy fold his money that way?"

"No. He used a billfold."

Qwilleran turned his head suddenly. "Koko! Get away from that lamp!"

The cat had crept onto the table and was rubbing his jaw against the wick regulator of the lamp decorated with pink roses. At the same moment Qwilleran felt a flicker of awareness in the same old place, and he smoothed his moustache with the stem of his pipe.

"Mary," he said, "who were the people who were coming to look at the light fixture?"

"I don't know. Andy merely said a woman from the suburbs was bringing her husband to approve it before she bought it."

Qwilleran leaned forward in his Morris chair. "Mary, if Andy was getting the chandelier down from the ceiling when he fell, it means that the customers had already okayed it! Andy was getting the thing down so they could take it with them! Don't you see? If the accident was genuine, it means the suburban couple were in the store when it happened. Why didn't they call the police? Who were they? Were they there at all? And if not, who *was* there?"

Mary looked guilty again. "I guess it's all right to tell you—now. . . . When I went to Andy's shop to apologize, I went twice. The first time I peeked in and saw him talking with someone, so I made a hasty retreat and tried against later."

"Did you recognize the person?"

"Yes, but I was afraid to let anyone know I had seen anything."

"What did you see, Mary?"

"I saw them arguing—Andy and C.C. And I was afraid C.C. might have seen *me*. You have no idea how relieved I was when I heard about his accident this morning. That's a terrible thing to say, I know."

"And you've been living in fear of that guy! Did he give you any reason to be?"

"Not actually, but . . . that's when the mysterious phone calls started."

"I knew it!" Qwilleran said. "I knew there was something fishy about that call the other night. How often—?"

"About once a week—always the same voice—obviously disguised. It sounded like a stage whisper—raspy—asthmatic."

"What was said?"

"Always something stupid and melodramatic. Vague hints about Andy's death. Vague predictions of danger. Now that C.C. is gone, I have a feeling the calls will stop."

"Don't be too sure," Qwilleran said. "There was a third person in Andy's shop that night—the owner of that twenty dollar bill. C.C. used a billfold and filed his currency flat. Someone else . . . I wonder how Ben Nicholas folds his money?"

"Qwill—"

"Would a woman ever fold a bill lengthwise?"

"Qwill," she said earnestly, "you're not serious about this, are you? I don't want any official interest to be revived in Andy's death." She said it bluntly and confronted him squarely.

"Why do you say that?"

Her eyes wavered. "Suppose you continued to investigate . . . and suppose you found an answer that pointed to murder . . . you would report it, wouldn't you?"

"Of course."

"And there would be a trial."

Qwilleran nodded.

"And because I found the body, I would have to testify, wouldn't I? And then my position would be exposed!" She slid out of the rocking chair and knelt on the floor at his side. "Qwill, that would be the end of everything I live for! The publicity—my father—you know what would happen!"

He put aside his pipe, and it fell on the floor. He studied her face.

"It's the newspapers I'm afraid of!" she said. "You know how they are about *names*. Anything for a *name!* Leave matters the way they are," she begged. "Andy's gone. Nothing will bring him back. Don't make any more inquiries. Qwill. Please!" She reached for his hands and stared at him with eyes wide and pleading. "Please do it for me." She bent her head and rubbed her smooth cheek against the back of his hand, and Qwilleran quickly raised her face to his.

"Please, Qwill, tell me you'll drop the whole matter."

"Mary, I don't . . ."

"Qwill, please promise." Her lips were very close. There was a breathless moment. Time stood still.

Then they heard: *"Grrrowrrr . . . yeowww!"*

Then a hissing: *"Hhhhhhh!"*

"Grrrowrrr! Owf!"

"KOKO!" shouted the man.

"Ak-ak-ak-ak-ak!"

"Yum Yum!"

"GRRRRR!"

"Koko, *quit* that!"

SIXTEEN

Qwilleran dreamed about Niagara Falls that night, and when the tumult of the cataract succeeded in waking him, he glanced about wildly in his darkened room. There was a roar of water—a rushing, raging torrent. Then, with a gasp and a choking groan, it stopped.

He sat up in his swan bed and listened. In a moment it started again, somewhat less deafening than in his dream—a gushing, swishing whirlpool, followed by a snort, a shuddering groan, a few final sobs, and silence.

Gradually the source of the noise penetrated his

sleep-drugged mind. Plumbing! The aged plumbing of an old house! But why was it flushing in the night? Qwilleran swung his legs out of bed and staggered to the bathroom.

He switched on the light. There, balancing on the edge of the baroque bathtub, was Koko, with one paw on the porcelain lever of the old-fashioned toilet, watching the swirling water with an intent, near-sighted gaze. Yum Yum was sitting in the marble washbowl, blinking her eyes at the sudden brightness. Once more Koko stepped on the lever and stared in fascination as the water cascaded, churned, gurgled, and disappeared.

"You monkey!" Qwilleran said. "How did you discover that gadget?" He was unsure whether to be peeved at the interruption of his sleep or proud of the cat's mechanical aptitude. He lugged Koko, squalling and writhing, from the bathroom and tossed him on the cushions of the Morris chair. "What were you trying to do? Resurrect Yum Yum's mouse?"

Koko licked his rumpled fur as if it had been contaminated by something indescribably offensive.

Daylight in a menacing yellow-gray began to creep over the winter sky, devising new atrocities in the form of weather. While opening a can of minced clams for the cats, Qwilleran planned his day. For one thing, he wanted to find out how Ben Nicholas folded his money. He also wished he knew how that red feather had transferred from a tweed porkpie to a silk tophat. He had asked Koko about it, and

Koko had merely squeezed one eye. As for the avalanche, Qwilleran had discussed it with Mary, and she had a glib explanation: "Well, you see, the attic in Ben's building is used for sleeping rooms, and it's heated."

He had not exactly promised Mary that he would drop his unofficial investigation. He had been on the verge of promising when Koko created that commotion. Afterwards, Qwilleran had simply said, "Trust me, Mary. I won't do anything to hurt you," and she had become nicely emotional, and altogether it had been a gratifying evening. She had even accepted his Christmas Eve invitation. She said she would go to the Press Club as Mary Duxbury—not as Mary Duckworth, junk dealer—because the society writers would recognize her.

Qwilleran still faced a dilemma, however. To drop his investigation was to shirk his own idea of responsibility; to pursue it was to hurt Junktown, and this neglected stepchild of City Hall needed a champion, not another antagonist.

By the time the junk shops opened and Qwilleran started his rounds, the weather had devised another form of discomfort: a clammy cold that chilled the bones and hovered over Junktown like a musty dishrag.

He went first to Bit o' Junk, but Ben's shop was closed.

Then he tried the store that sold tech-tiques, and for the first time since Qwilleran had arrived in Junktown, the place was open. When he walked in,

Hollis Prantz came loping from the stockroom in the rear, wearing something somber and carrying a paintbrush.

"Just varnishing some display cabinets," he explained. "Getting ready for the big day tomorrow."

"Don't let me interrupt you," Qwilleran said, as he perused the shop in mystification. He saw tubes from fifteen-year-old television sets, early hand-wired circuits, prehistoric radio parts, and old-fashioned generator cutouts from 1935 automobiles. "Just tell me one thing," he said. "Do you expect to make a living from this stuff?"

"Nobody makes a living in this business," said Prantz. "We all need another source of income."

"Or extreme monastic tastes," Qwilleran added.

"I happen to have a little rental property, and I'm semi-retired. I had a heart attack last year, and I'm taking it easy."

"You're young to have a thing like that happen." Qwilleran guessed the dealer was in his early forties.

"You're lucky if you get a warning early in life. It's my theory that Cobb had a heart attack when he was tearing that building apart; that's heavy work for a man of his age."

"What kind of work did you do—before this?"

"I was in paint and wallpaper." The dealer said it almost apologetically. "Not much excitement in the paint business, but I get a real charge out of this new shop of mine."

"What gave you the idea for tech-tiques?"

"Wait till I get rid of this varnish brush." In a second Prantz was back with an old straight-back office chair. "Here. Have a seat."

Qwilleran studied the disassembled innards of a primitive typewriter. "You'll have to talk fast to convince me this junk is going to catch on."

The dealer smiled. "Well, I'll tell you. People will collect anything today, because there aren't enough good antiques to go around. They make lamps out of worm-eaten fence posts. They frame twenty-year-old burlesque posters. Why not preserve the fragments of the early automotive and electronics industry?" Prantz shifted to a confidential tone. "I've got a promotion I'm working on, based on a phenomenon of our times—the acceleration of obsolescence. My idea is to accelerate antiquity. The sooner an item goes out of style, the quicker it makes its comeback as a collector's piece. It used to be a hundred years before discards made the grade as collectibles. Now it's thirty. I intend to speed it up to twenty or even fifteen. . . . Don't write this up," the dealer added hastily. "It's still in the thinking stage. Protect me, like a good fellow."

Qwilleran shrank into his overcoat when he left Hollis Prantz. The dealer had changed a five for him—with dollar bills folded crosswise—but there was something about Prantz that did not ring true.

"Mr. Qwilleran! Mr. Qwilleran!"

Running footsteps came up behind him, and he turned to catch an armful of brown corduroy, opossum fur, notebooks, and flying blond hair.

Ivy, the youngest of the three sisters, was out of

breath. "Just got off the bus," she panted. "Had a life class this morning. Are you on your way to our shop?"

"No, I'm heading for Mrs. McGuffey's."

"Don't go there! 'Mrs. McGuffey is too damn stuffy!' That's what Cluthra says."

"Business is business, Ivy. Are you all ready for Christmas?"

"Guess what! I'm getting an easel for Christmas! A real painter's easel."

"I'm glad I ran into you," Qwilleran said. "I'd like to decorate my apartment for the holidays, but I don't have your artistic touch. Besides, this tricky knee—"

"I'd love to help you. Do you want an old-fashioned Christmas tree or something swinging?"

"A tree would last about three minutes at my place. I have a couple of cats, and they're airborne most of the time. But I thought I could get some ropes of greens at Lombardo's—"

"I've got a staple gun at the shop. I can do it right now."

When Ivy arrived at Qwilleran's apartment, the cedar garlands—ten dollars' worth—were heaped in the middle of the floor, being circled warily by Koko and Yum Yum. The latter left for parts unknown at the sight of the blond visitor, but Koko sat tall and watched her carefully as if she were not to be trusted.

Qwilleran offered Ivy a Coke before she started decorating, and she sat in the rocking chair made of twigs, her straight blond hair falling like a cape over her shoulders. As she talked, her little-girl mouth pouted and pursed and broke into winning smiles.

Qwilleran asked, "Where did you three sisters get such unusual names?"

"Don't you know? They're different kinds of art glass. My mother was madly Art Nouveau. I'd rather be called Kim or Leslie. When I'm eighteen I'm going to change my name and move to Paris to study art. I mean, when I get the money my mother left me—if my sisters haven't used it all up," she added with a frown. "They're my legal guardians."

"You seem to have a lot of fun together in that shop."

Ivy hesitated. "Not really. They're kind of mean to me. Cluthra won't let me go steady . . . and Amberina is trying to suppress my talent. She wants me to study bookkeeping or nursing or something *grim* like that."

"Who's giving you the magnificent Christmas present?"

"What?"

"The easel."

"Oh! Well . . . I'm getting that from Tom. He's Amberina's husband. He's real neat. I think he's secretly in love with me, but don't *say* anything to anybody."

"Of course not. I'm flattered," said Qwilleran, "that you feel you can confide in me. What do you think about all the mishaps in Junktown? Are they as accidental as they appear?"

"Cluthra says the Dragon dropped that thing on her foot on purpose. Cluthra may decide to sue her for an enormous amount of money. *Five thousand dollars!*"

"An astronomical figure," Qwilleran agreed. "But what about the two recent deaths in Junktown?"

"Poor C.C.! He was a creep, but I felt sorry for him. His wife wasn't nice to him at all. Did you know she murdered her first husband? Of course, nobody could ever prove it."

"And Andy. Did you know Andy?"

"He was dreamy. I was mad about Andy. Wasn't that a horrible way to die?"

"Do you think he might have been murdered?"

Ivy's eyes grew wide with delight at the possibility. "Maybe the Dragon—"

"But Mary Duckworth was in love with Andy. She wouldn't do a thing like that."

The girl thought about it for a few seconds. "She couldn't be in love with him," she announced. "She's a witch! Cluthra says so! And everybody knows witches can't fall in love."

"I must say you have a colorful collection of characters in Junktown. What do you know about Russell Patch?"

"I used to like him before he bleached his hair. I kind of think he's mixed up in some kind of racket, like—I don't know . . . "

"Who's his roommate?"

"Stan's hairdresser at Skyline Towers. You know all those rich widows and kept women that live there? They tell Stan all their secrets and give him fabulous presents. He does Cluthra's hair. She pretends it's natural, but you should see how *gray* it is when it starts to grow out."

"Sylvia Katzenhide lives in the same building, doesn't she?"

The girl nodded and reflected. "Cluthra says she'd be a brilliant success at blackmail. Sylvia's got something on everybody."

"Including Ben Nicholas and Hollis Prantz?"

"I don't know." Ivy sipped her Coke while she toyed with the possibilities. "But I think Ben's a dope addict. I haven't decided about the other one. He may be some kind of pervert."

Later, when the garlands were festooned on the fireplace wall and Ivy had departed with her staple gun, Qwilleran said to Koko: "Out of the mouths of babes come the damnedest fabrications!" Furthermore, the experiment had cost him ten dollars, and the decorations only served to enshrine the bad-dispositioned old lady hanging over the fireplace. He determined to substitute the Mackintosh coat of arms as soon as he could get some assistance in hoisting it to the mantel.

Before going downtown to hand in his copy, he made two phone calls and wangled some invitations. He told Cluthra he wanted to see how antique dealers live, what they collect, how they furnish their apartments. He told Russell Patch he had a Siamese cat who was crazy about music. And he told Ben he wanted to have the firsthand experience of scrounging. He also asked him to change a five-dollar bill.

"Alas," said Ben, "if we could change a fin, we would retire from this wretched business."

At the *Daily Fluxion* that afternoon Qwilleran walked into the Feature Department with its even rows of modern metal desks that had always looked so orderly and serene, and suddenly he found the scene cold, sterile, monotonous, and without character.

Arch Riker said, "Did you see how we handled the auction story in today's paper? The boss liked your copy."

"The whole back page! That was more than I expected," Qwilleran said, tossing some triple-spaced sheets on the desk. "Here's the second installment, and I'll have more tomorrow. This morning I interviewed a man who sells some absurd junk called tech-tiques."

"Rosie told me about him. He's new in Junktown."

"He's either out of his mind or pulling a hoax. In fact, I think Hollis Prantz is a fraud. He claims to have a weak heart, but you should have seen him running up stairs two at a time! I'm discovering all kinds of monkeyshines in Junktown."

"Don't get sidetracked," Riker advised him. "Bear down on the writing."

"But, Arch! I've unearthed some good clues in the Andy Glanz case! I also have my suspicions about Cobb's death."

"For Pete's sake, Qwill, the police called them accidents. Let's leave it that way."

"That's one reason I'm suspicious. Everyone in Junktown is busy explaining that the two deaths were accidents. They protest too much."

"I can understand their position," Riker told him. "If Junktown gets a reputation as a high-crime neighborhood, the junkers will stay away in droves. . . . Look here, I've got five pages to lay out. I can't argue with you all day."

"If there's been a crime committed, it should be exposed," Qwilleran persisted.

"All right," said Riker. "If you want to investigate, go ahead. But do it on your time and wait until after Christmas. The way your antique series is shaping up, you've got a good chance to win first prize."

By the time Qwilleran returned to Junktown, Ivy had spread the word that he was a private detective operating with two evil-eyed Siamese cats who were trained to attack.

"Is it true?" asked the young man in sideburns and dark glasses at the Junque Trunque.

"Is it true?" asked the woman who ran the shop called Nuthin' But Chairs.

"I wish it were," Qwilleran said. "I'm just a newspaperman, doing a job that isn't very glamorous."

She half closed her eyes. "I see you as a Yorkshire Windsor. Everyone resembles some kind of chair. That dainty little Sheraton is a ballet dancer. That English Chippendale looks just like my landlord. You're a Yorkshire Windsor. . . . Think about it for a while, and all your friends will turn into chairs."

After listening to this woman's conversation and Ivy's speculations and Hollis Prantz's dubious theories, Qwilleran was relieved to meet Mrs. McGuffey. She seemed to be a sensible sort.

He asked about the name of her shop, and she explained, "They're all wooden containers. The noggin has a handle like a cup. The piggin has a stave, and it's used as a dipper. The firkin is for storage."

"Where do you get your information?"

"From books. When I have no customers, I sit here and read. Nice work for a retired schoolteacher. If there's any book on American history or antiques that you'd like to borrow, just ask."

"Do you have anything on the history of Junktown? I'm especially curious about the Cobb mansion."

"Most important house on our street! Built by William Towne Spencer, the famous abolitionist, in 1855. He had two younger brothers, James and Philip, who built smaller replicas next door. Also a spinster sister, Mathilda, blind from birth and killed at the age of thirty-two when she fell down the stairs of her brother's house." She spoke with an authority that Qwilleran welcomed. He had had his fill of hearsay and addled theories.

"I've noticed that Junktown residents are prone to fall and kill themselves," he said. "Strange that it started way back when."

The dealer shook her head mournfully. "Poor Mrs. Cobb! I wonder if she'll be able to continue running the shop without her husband."

"He was the sparkplug of Junktown, they tell me."

"Probably true . . . but confidentially, I abhorred the man. He had no manners! You don't act that way in a civilized society. In my opinion the real loss to the community was Andrew Glanz. A fine young man, with great promise, and a real scholar! I say this with pride, because it was I who taught him to read—twenty-five years ago, up north in Boyerville. My, he was a smart boy! And a good speller. I knew he would turn out to be a writer." The lines in her face were radiant.

"He wrote features on antiques?"

"Yes, but he was also writing a novel, about which I have mixed emotions. He gave me the first ten chapters to read. I refrained from discouraging him, naturally, but . . . I'm afraid I do not approve of today's sordid fiction. And yet that is what sells, they say."

"What was the setting of Andy's novel?"

"The setting was authentic—a community of antique dealers similar to ours—but the story involved all sorts of unsavory characters: alcoholics, gamblers, homosexuals, prostitutes, dope peddlers, adulterers!" Mrs. McGuffey shuddered. "Oh, dear! If our street were anything like that book, I believe I would close up shop tomorrow!"

Qwilleran stroked his moustache. "You don't think there's anything like that going on in Junktown?"

"Oh, no! Nothing at all! Except . . ." She lowered

her voice and glanced toward a customer who had wandered into the store. "I wouldn't want you to repeat this, but . . . they say that the little old man at the fruit stand is a bookkeeper."

"You mean a bookmaker? He takes bets?"

"That's what they *say*. Please don't put it in the paper. This is a respectable neighborhood."

The customer interrupted. "Excuse me. Do you have any butter molds?"

"Just one moment," the dealer said with a gracious smile, "and I'll be glad to help you."

"What happened to Andy's manuscript?" Qwilleran asked as he headed for the door.

"I believe he gave it to his friend, Miss Duckworth. She was begging to see it, *but*," Mrs. McGuffey concluded triumphantly, "he wanted his old schoolmarm to read it first."

SEVENTEEN

With savage glee the humidity decided to turn into a cold ugly rain. Qwilleran hurried to The Blue Dragon as fast as his knee would permit.

"I'm going to do some illegal scrounging tonight," he announced to Mary Duckworth. "Ben Nicholas is going to show me the ropes."

"Where is he taking you?"

"To an old theatre on Zwinger Street. He said it's boarded up, but he knows how to get in through the stage door. All I want is the experience, so I can write a piece about the preservationists who risk arrest to salvage historic architectural fragments. I think the practice should be publicized with a view to having it sanctioned."

Mary beamed her admiration for him. "Qwill, you're talking like a confirmed junker! You've been converted!"

"I know a good story when I see one, that's all. Meanwhile, would you mind lending me the manuscript of Andy's novel? Mrs. McGuffey was telling me about it, and since it's all about Junktown—"

"Manuscript? I have no manuscript."

"Mrs. McGuffey said—"

"Andy allowed me to read the first chapter, that was all."

"What happened to it, then?"

"I have no idea. Robert Maus would know."

"Will you phone him?"

"Now?"

Qwilleran nodded impatiently.

She glanced at the tall-case clock. "This is an inconvenient time to call. He'll be preparing dinner. Is it really so urgent?"

Nevertheless, she dialed the number.

"William," she said, "may I speak with Mr. Maus? . . . Please tell him it's Mary Duxbury. . . . That's what I was afraid of. Just a moment." She turned to Qwilleran. "The houseboy says Bob is making hollandaise for the kohlrabi and can't be interrupted."

"Tell him the *Daily Fluxion* is about to print a vile rumor about one of his clients."

The attorney came to the telephone (Qwilleran

could visualize him, wearing an apron, holding a dripping spoon) and said he knew nothing about a manuscript; nothing had turned up among the papers of the Andrew Glanz estate.

"Then where is it?" Qwilleran asked Mary. "Do you suppose it was destroyed—by someone who had reason to want it suppressed? What was in the chapter that you read?"

"It was about a woman who was plotting to poison her husband. It immediately captured one's interest."

"Why didn't Andy let you read more?"

"He was quite secretive about his novel. Don't you think most writers are sensitive about their work before it's published?"

"Perhaps all the characters were drawn from life. Mrs. McGuffey seemed to think they were wildly imaginary, but I doubt whether she's in a position to know. She's lived a sheltered life. Perhaps Andy's story exposed a few Junktown secrets that would prove embarrassing—or incriminating."

"He wouldn't have done anything like that! Andy was so considerate—"

Qwilleran clenched his teeth. So considerate, so honest, so clever, so intelligent. He knew it by heart. "Perhaps you were in the story, too," he told Mary. "Perhaps that's why Andy wouldn't let you read farther. You may have been so transparently disguised that your position would be revealed and your family would crack down on you."

Mary's eyes flashed. "No! Andy would never have been so unkind."

"Well, we'll never know now!" Qwilleran started to leave and then turned back. "You know this Hollis Prantz. He says he used to be in the paint and wallpaper business and he retired because of a weak heart, and yet he's as agile as a fox. He was varnishing display cases when I was there today—"

"Varnishing?" Mary asked.

"He said he was getting ready for the Block Party tomorrow, and yet he has very little merchandise to offer."

"Varnishing on a day like this? It will never dry! If you varnish in damp weather, it remains sticky forever."

"Are you sure?"

"It's a fact. You may think it's dry, but whenever the humidity is high, the surface becomes tacky again."

Qwilleran huffed into his moustache. "Strange mistake to make, isn't it?"

"For someone who claims he's been in the paint business," Mary said, "it's an incredible mistake!"

Later, the rain turned to a treacherous wet snow as fine as fog, and Qwilleran went to a cheap clothing store in the neighborhood to buy a red hunting cap with earflaps. He also borrowed the Cobb flashlight and crowbar in preparation for his scrounging debut.

But first he had an invitation to drop in on Russell Patch at the cocktail hour to hear the twenty thousand dollar sound system. He went home and trussed Koko in the blue harness. The leash had unaccountably disappeared, but it was not necessary for a social call. The harness alone made Koko look trim and professional, and it afforded a good grip while Qwilleran was carrying the cat down the street.

"This trip," he explained to his purring accomplice, "is not purely in the pursuit of culture. I want you to nose around and see if you can turn up anything significant."

The carriage house was two doors away, and Qwilleran tucked Koko inside his overcoat to keep him dry. They entered through the refinishing shop, and their host led them up a narrow staircase to a dazzling apartment. The floor was a checkerboard of large black and white tiles, and a dozen white marble statues on white pedestals were silhouetted against the walls, some of which were painted dull black, some shiny red.

Russell introduced his roommate, a sallow young man who was either shy or furtive and who wore on his finger a diamond of spectacular brilliance, and Qwilleran introduced Koko, who was now riding on his shoulder. Koko regarded the two strangers briefly and dismissed them at once by turning and staring in the opposite direction.

The music that filled the room was the busy kind of fiddling and tootling that made Qwilleran nervous. It came at him from all directions."

"Do you like baroque music?" Russ asked. "Or would you prefer another type?"

"Koko prefers something more soothing," Qwilleran replied.

"Stan, put on that Schubert sonata."

The sound system occupied a bank of old kitchen cabinets transformed into an Italian Renaissance breakfront, and Koko immediately checked it out.

"Stan, make us a drink," Russell ordered. "Say, that cat isn't vicious at all. I heard he was a wild one!"

"If you also heard that I'm a private eye, it's a lie," said Qwilleran.

"Glad of that. I'd hate to see anyone loafing around Junktown digging up dirt. We've worked hard to build a good image here."

"I dug up an interesting fact, however. I learned your friend Andy was writing a novel about Junktown."

"Oh, sure," said Russ. "I told him he was wasting his time. Unless you dish out a lot of sex, who buys novels?"

"Maybe he did just that. Had you read the manuscript?"

Russ laughed. "No, but I can guess what it was like. Andy was a prune, a real prune."

"The funny thing is that the manuscript has disappeared."

"He probably scrapped it. I told you how he was—a perfectionist."

Qwilleran accepted the ginger ale he had requested and said to Stan, "Are you in the antique business?"

"I'm a hairdresser," Stan said quietly.

"A lucrative field, I hear."

"I do all right."

Russ volunteered, "If you want to know what really keeps him in Jaguars and diamonds, he plays the stock market."

"Are you interested in the market?" Stan asked the newsman.

"To tell the truth, I've never had anything to invest, so I've never made a study of it."

"You don't have to know much," Stan said. "You can go in for no-load mutuals or do like me. I have a discretionary account, and my broker doubles my money every year."

"You mean that?" Qwilleran lighted his pipe thoughtfully. He was making a computation. If he won one of the *Fluxion*'s top prizes, he could run it up to . . . two, four, eight, sixteen, thirty-two thousand in five years. Perhaps, after all, he was wasting his time trying to make murders out of molehills.

As for Koko, he had checked the place out and was now lounging near a heat register, ignoring the Schubert.

"Say, I'd like to try something," Russ said. "I've got some electronic music that hits the high frequencies—white noise, computer music, synthesized sound, and all that. Let's see if the cat reacts. Animals can hear things beyond the human range."

"Okay with me" Qwilleran said.

The Schubert came to an end, and then the thirty-six speakers gave out a concert of whines and whinnies, blats and bleeps, flutterings and tweeterings that baffled the eardrums. At the first squawk Koko pricked up his ears, and in a moment he was on his feet. He looked bewildered. He ran across the room, changed course and dashed back erratically.

"He doesn't like it," Qwilleran protested.

The music slid into a series of hollow whispers and echoes, with pulsing vibrations. Koko raced across the room and threw himself against the wall.

"You'd better turn it off!"

"This is great!" Russ said. "Stan, did you ever see anything like this?"

From the speakers came an unearthly screech. Koko rose in the air, faster than the eye could register, and landed on top of the stereo cabinets.

"Turn it off!" Qwilleran shouted above the din.

It was too late. Koko had swooped down again, landing on Russ Patch's head, digging in with his claws, until the bellow that came from the man's throat sent him flying through space.

Russ touched his hand to his temple and found blood.

"Serves you right," said Stan quietly, as he flipped the switch on the stereo.

Moments later, when Qwilleran took Koko home, the cat was outwardly calm, but the man could feel his trembling.

"Sorry, old boy," he said. "That was a dirty trick."

He carried Koko back to his apartment and set him gently on the floor. Yum Yum came running to touch noses, but Koko ignored her. He had a long drink of water, then stood on his hind legs and clawed Qwilleran's trousers. The man picked him up and walked the floor with him until it was time to leave for his next appointment.

Locking the cats in the apartment, he started for the stairway, but the long forlorn howl behind the closed door tore at his heart. As he went slowly down the stairs, the cries became louder and more piteous, and all Qwilleran's regrets about Koko's self-sufficiency vanished. The cat needed him. Inwardly elated, Qwilleran returned and gathered up his eager friend and took him to call on Cluthra.

EIGHTEEN

With enticing interrogatives in her voice Cluthra
had invited Qwilleran to come later (?) in the
evening (?) when they could both relax (?). But he
had pleaded another engagement and had played
dumb to her innuendos.

Now at the discreet hour of seven thirty he and
Koko took a taxi to Skyline Towers and a swift elevator to the seventeenth floor. Koko did not object
to elevators that ascended—only the kind that sank
beneath him.

Cluthra met them in a swirling cloud of pale green
chiffon and ostrich feathers. "I didn't know you

were bringing a friend," she said with her husky laugh.

"Koko has had a bad experience this evening, and he didn't want me to leave him." Qwilleran told her about Russell's cruel experiment with electronic music.

"Beware of young men dressed in white!" she said. "They've got something they're hiding."

She ushered him into the cozy living room, which was done entirely in matching paisley—paisley fabric on the walls, paisley draperies, paisley slipcovers—all in warm tones of beige, brown and gold. The fabric gave the room the stifling hush of a closed coffin. Music was playing softly—something passionate, with violins. Cluthra's perfume was overpowering.

Qwilleran looked around him at the polliwogs that characterize the paisley pattern and tried to estimate their number. Ten thousand? A hundred thousand? Half a million?

"Will you have a drinkie?" Cluthra extended the invitation with a conspiratorial gleam in her green eyes.

"Just a club soda. No liquor. Heavy on the ice."

"Honey, I can do better than that for my favorite newspaper reporter," she said, and when the drink came, it was pink, sparkling, and heavily aromatic.

Qwilleran sniffed it and frowned.

"Homemade chokecherry syrup," she explained. "Men like it because it's bitter."

He took a cautious sip. The taste was not bad. Pleasant, in fact. "Did you make it?"

"Lordy, no! One of my kooky customers. She's made a study of medicinal weeds, and she does this stuff with juniper, lovage, mullein, and I don't know what else. Mullein puts hair on your chest, lover," Cluthra added with a wink.

Qwilleran had taken a seat in a stiff pull-up chair, with Koko huddled on his lap.

"You've picked the only backbreaking chair in the place," she protested. She herself was now seductively arranged on the paisley sofa surrounded by paisley pillows, carefully concealing her walking cast with the folds of her chiffon gown. Yards of ostrich fluff framed her shoulders, cascaded down her hilly slopes and circled the hem.

She patted the sofa cushions. "Why don't you sit over here and be comfy?"

"With this cranky knee I'm better off on a straight chair," Qwilleran said, and it was more or less true.

Cluthra regarded him with fond accusation. "You've been kidding us," she said. "You're not really a newspaper reporter. But we like you just the same."

"If your kid sister has been spreading stories, forget it," he said. "I'm just an underpaid, overworked feature writer for the *Fluxion*, with a private curiosity about sudden deaths. Ivy has a wild imagination."

"It's just a phase she's going through."

"By the way, did you know Andy was writing a novel about Junktown?"

"When Andy came over here," she said, relishing the memory, "we did very little talking about literature."

"Do you know Hollis Prantz very well?"

Cluthra rolled her eyes. "Preserve me from men who wear gray button-front sweaters!"

Qwilleran gulped his iced drink. The apartment was warm, and Koko was like a fur lap robe. But as they talked, the cat relaxed and eventually slid to the floor, much to the man's relief. Soon Koko disappeared against the protective coloration of the beige and brown paisley. Qwilleran mopped his brow. He was beginning to suffocate. The temperature seemed to be in the nineties, and the polliwogs dazzled his eyes. He could look down at the plain beige carpet and see polliwogs; he could look up at the white ceiling and see polliwogs. He closed his eyes.

"Do you feel all right, honey?"

"Yes, I feel fine. My eyes are tired, that's all. And it's a trifle warm in here."

"Would you like to lie down? You look kind of groggy. Come and lie down on the sofa."

Qwilleran contemplated the inviting picture before him—the deep-cushioned sofa, the soft pillows. He also caught a glimpse of movement behind Cluthra's halo of red hair. Koko had risen silently and almost invisibly to the back of the sofa.

"Take off your coat and lie down and make yourself comfy," his hostess was urging. "You don't

have to mind your manners with Cousin Cluthra."
She gave his moustache and shoulders an apprecia-
tive appraisal and batted her lashes.

Qwilleran wished he had not come. He liked
women who were more subtle. He hated paisley. His
eyes had been bothering him lately (maybe he
needed glasses) and the allover pattern was making
him dizzy. Or was it the drink? He wondered about
that cherry syrup. Juniper, mullein, *lovage*. What the
devil was lovage?

Then without warning Cluthra sneezed. "Oh! Excuse me!"

Qwilleran took the opportunity to change the
subject. "They'll be burying old C.C. tomorrow," he
said with an attempt at animation, although he had
an overwhelming desire to close his eyes.

"He was a real man," Cluthra said with narrowed
eyes. "You don't find many of them any more, believe me!" She sneezed again. "Excuse me! I don't
know what's the matter with me."

Qwilleran could guess. Koko had his nose buried
in her ostrich feathers. "Iris is taking it very hard,"
he said.

Cluthra pulled a chiffon handkerchief from some
hidden place and touched her eyes, which were red-
dening and beginning to stream. "Iris wod't have
ady bore ghostly problebs with her glasses," she
said. "C.C. used to get up id the dight to play tricks
with theb."

"That's what I call devotion," Qwilleran said.

"Look here! Are you by any chance allergic to cat hair?"

The visit ended abruptly, and it was with a great sense of escape that Qwilleran got out in the cold air and shook the polliwogs from his vision.

Cluthra had called after him, "You bust visit be without your buddy dext tibe."

He took Koko home and got into his scrounging clothes for his next appointment. But first he looked up a word in the dictionary. "Lovage—a domestic remedy." For what ailment or deficiency, the book did not say. Qwilleran also opened a can of shrimp and gave Koko a treat, and he spent a certain amount of time thinking about Cluthra's voice. Whiskey voice, they used to call it.

At the appointed hour he found Ben waiting at the curb in a gray station wagon that was a masterpiece of rust, with a wire coat hanger serving as a radio antenna and with the curbside headlight, anchored by a single screw, staring glumly at the gutter. The driver was bundled up in a mackinaw, early aviator's helmet, and long striped muffler.

The motor coughed a few times, the car shuddered and lurched away from the curb, sucking up blasts of icy cold and dampness through a gaping hole under the dashboard. Fortunately it was a short drive to the Garrick Theatre in the demolition area. It stood proudly among other abandoned buildings, looking like a relic of fifteenth century Venice.

"Alas, poor Garrick! We knew it well," said Ben morosely. "The great and glorious names of the theatre once played here. Then . . . vaudeville. Then silent pictures. Then talkies. Then double features. Then Italian films. Then horror movies. Then nothing. And now—only Benjamin X. Nicholas, playing to a ghostly audience and applauded by pigeons."

Qwilleran carried the crowbar. They both carried flashlights, and Ben directed the newsman in wrenching the boarding from the stage door. The boards came away easily, as if accustomed to cooperating, and the two men entered the dark, silent, empty building.

Ben led the way down a narrow hall, past the doorkeeper's cubicle, past the skeleton of an iron staircase, and onto the stage. The auditorium was a hollow shell, dangling with dead wires, coated with dust, and raw in patches where decorations had been pried from the sidewalls and the two tiers of boxes. Qwilleran beamed his light at the ceiling; all that remained of the Garrick's grandeur were the frescoes in the dome—floating images of Romeo and Juliet, Antony and Cleopatra. If there was nothing left to scrounge, why had Ben brought him here? Soon Qwilleran guessed the answer. The old actor had taken center stage, and an eerie performance began.

"Friends, Romans, countrymen—" Ben declaimed in passionate tones.

"Friends, Romans—" came a distant reverberating voice.

"Lend me your ears!" said Ben.

"Countrymen—friends, Romans—lend me—

countrymen—ears—lend me," whispered the ghosts of old actors.

"Alas," said Ben when he had spoken the speech and Qwilleran had applauded with gloved thumps and a bravo or two. "Alas, we were born too late. . . . But let us to work! What does our heart desire? A bit of carving? A crumb of marble! Not much choice; the wretches have raped the place. But here!" He kicked a heating grille. "A bronze bauble for your pleasure!"

The moldings crumbled, and the newsman easily pried the blackened grillwork loose. The dust rose. Both men coughed and choked. There was a whirring of wings in the darkness overhead, and Qwilleran thought of bats.

"Let's get out of here," he said.

"But stay! One more treasure!" said Ben, flashing his light around the tiers of boxes. All but one of them had been denuded of embellishment. The first box on the left still bore its sculptured crest supported by cherubs blowing trumpets and wearing garlands of flowers. "It would bring a pretty penny."

"How much?"

"A hundred dollars from any dealer. Two hundred from a smart collector. Three hundred from some bloody fool."

"How would we get it off?"

"Others have succeeded. Let us be bold!"

Ben led the way to the mezzanine level and into the box.

"You hold both lights," Qwilleran told him, "and I'll see what I can do with the crowbar."

The newsman leaned over the railing and pried at the carving. The floor of the box creaked.

"Lay on, Macduff!" cried Ben.

"Shine the light over the railing," Qwilleran instructed. "I'm working in shadow." Then he paused with crowbar in midair. He had seen something in the dust on the floor. He turned to look at Ben and was blinded by the two flashlights. A shudder in his moustache made him plunge to the rear of the box. There was a wrenching of timbers and a crash and a cloud of choking dust rising from the floor below. Two beams of light danced crazily on the walls and ceiling.

"What the hell happened?" gasped Qwilleran. "The railing let loose!"

The railing was gone, and the sagging floor of the box sloped off into blackness.

"The saints were with us!" cried Ben, choked with emotion or dust.

"Give me a light and let's get out of here," said the newsman.

They drove back to Junktown with the brass grille in the back seat, Qwilleran silent as he recalled his narrow escape and what he had seen in the dust.

"Our performance lacked fire this evening," Ben apologized. An icicle glistened on the tip of his nose. "We were frozen to the bone. But come to the pub and witness a performance that will gladden your heart. Come join us in a brandy."

The Lion's Tail had been a neighborhood bank in the 1920s—a miniature Roman temple, now desecrated by a neon sign and panels of glass blocks in the arched windows. Inside, it was lofty, undecorated, smoke-filled, and noisy. An assortment of patrons stood at the bar and filled half the tables—men in work clothes, and raggle-taggle members of Junktown's after-dark set.

As Ben made his entrance, he was greeted by cheering, stamping of feet, and pounding of tables. He acknowledged the acclaim graciously and held up his hand for silence.

"Tonight," he said, "a brief scene from *King Richard III*, and then drinks for the entire house!"

With magnificent poise he moved through the crowd, his muffler hanging down to his heels, and disappeared. A moment later he emerged on a small balcony.

"Now is the winter of our discontent . . ." he began.

The man had a ringing delivery, and the audience was quiet if not wholly attentive.

"He capers nimbly in a lady's chamber," came the voice from the balcony, and there was riotous laughter down below.

Ben concluded with a melodramatic leer: "I am determined to prove a villain and hate the idle pleasures of these days!"

The applause was deafening, the actor bowed humbly, and the bartender went to work filling glasses.

When Ben came down from the balcony, he threw a wad of folded bills on the bar—bills folded lengthwise. "King Richard or Charley's aunt, what matter?" he said to Qwilleran with a gloomy countenance. "The day of the true artist is gone forever. The baggy-pants comic is an 'artist.' So is the bullfighter, tightrope walker and long-haired guitar player. Next it will be baseball players and bricklayers! Sir, the time is out of joint."

The thirsty audience soon demanded an encore.

"Pardon us," Ben said to Qwilleran. "We must oblige," and he moved once more toward the balcony.

The newsman quietly left The Lion's Tail, wondering where Ben acquired the cash to buy the applause that he craved—and whether he had known that the box at the Garrick was a booby trap.

Qwilleran went home. He found the cats asleep on their cushions, which bent their whiskers into half smiles, and he retired to his own bed, his mind swimming with questions. What was Ben's racket? Was the actor as nutty as he appeared? Was his sudden affluence connected with the Ellsworth house? Ben had been there, Qwilleran was sure. He had seen the evidence in the dust—feathery arabesques made by the tassels of his muffler. Still, Ben's reception at The Lion's Tail indicated that his audience was accustomed to his largess.

The newsman remembered something Cobb had said. "The nearest Ben ever got to Broadway was Macy's toy department." Then a few minutes later

Cobb had contradicted himself. "Ben's got a bundle. He used to make big money." And at this remark Iris had glanced at her husband in surprise.

Did Ben have a shady sideline that supplied him with the money to bribe his audience into attention and applause? Did Cobb know about it? Qwilleran's answers were only guesses, as unprovable as they were improbable, and the questions kept him awake.

Deliberately he turned his mind to a more agreeable subject: Christmas Eve at the Press Club. He could picture the society writers—and Jack Jaunti— doing a double take when he walked in with Mary, and he could see the newshounds being outwardly casual but secretly impressed by the magic name of Duxbury. Qwilleran realized he ought to cap the evening with a Christmas gift for Mary, but what could he buy for the daughter of a millionaire?

Before he fell asleep, the answer spread over his consciousness like a warm blanket. It was a brilliant idea—so brilliant that he sat up in bed. And if the *Daily Fluxion* would cooperate, it would save Junktown.

Qwilleran made a mental note to call the managing editor the first thing in the morning, and then he slept, the pillow turning up one end of his moustache in a half-smile.

NINETEEN

Waking on Wednesday morning, Qwilleran was vaguely aware of a lump in his armpit. It was Yum Yum, hiding under the blankets in the safest spot she could find. But while she had run for cover, Koko was investigating the shattering noise that alarmed her. With his hind feet on a chair and his forepaws on the window sill, he was watching the pellets of ice that bounced off the panes of glass.

"Hailstorm!" Qwilleran groaned. "That's all we need to ruin the Block Party!"

Koko left the window and routed Yum Yum out of bed.

The hail sheathed the city in ice, but by eleven o'-clock that morning, the weather developed a conscience and the sun broke through. Junktown sparkled like a jewel. Buildings became crystal palaces. Utility wires, street signs, and traffic lights wore a glistening fringe of icicles, and even the trash cans were beautiful. It was the only decent gesture the weather had made all winter.

By noon the junkers were flocking into Zwinger Street. Angels flew from the lampposts, carolers were caroling, and Ben Nicholas in white beard and Santa Claus pantaloons held audience on the stoop in front of his shop. Tiny Spooner was there, taking pictures, and even the *Morning Rampage* had sent a photographer.

Qwilleran mixed with the crowd and eavesdropped in the shops, until it was time to return to the Junkery and take his turn at tending the shop. He found Cluthra on duty.

"This chair is *very* old," she was telling a customer. "It has the original milk paint. You'd better grab it. At twenty-seven fifty Mrs. Cobb isn't making a penny on it, I can guarantee. Why, on Cape Cod you'd have to pay sixty-five dollars!"

The customer capitulated, wrote a check, and left the shop in high glee, carrying a potty chair with sawed-off legs.

Cluthra turned the cashbox over to Qwilleran and explained the price tags. "Do you understand the code, hon?" she asked. "You read the numbers backwards to get the asking price, and then you can go up or down a few dollars, depending on the customer. Be careful of that banister-back chair; it has a loose leg. And don't forget, you're entitled to strangle every third customer who tells you about her grandmother."

The traffic in and out of the shop was heavy, but the buyers were less plentiful than the lookers and askers. Qwilleran decided to keep a log for Mrs. Cobb's benefit:

—Sold two blue glass things out of window, $18.50.

—Woman asked for Sheffield candlesticks.

—Man asked for horse brasses.

—Sold spool chest, $30.

—Kissed female customer and sold tin knife box, $35.

The customer in question had rushed at Qwilleran with a gay little shriek. "Qwill! What are you doing here?"

"Rosie Riker! How are you? You're looking great!" Actually she was looking matronly and somewhat ludicrous in her antiquing clothes.

"How've you been, Qwill? I keep telling Arch to bring you home to dinner. Mind if I sit down? I've been walking around for three hours."

"Not in the banister-back, Rosie. The leg's loose."

"I wish they'd turn those carol singers off for five minutes. How've you been, Qwill? What are you doing here?"

"Keeping shop while Mrs. Cobb's at her husband's funeral."

"You're looking fine. I'm glad you've still got that romantic moustache! Do you ever hear from Miriam?"

"Not directly, but my ex-mother-in-law puts the bite on me once in a while. Miriam's in that Connecticut sanitarium again."

"Don't let those vultures take advantage of you, Qwill. They're plenty well off."

"Well, how've you been, Rosie? Are you buying anything?"

"I'm looking for a Christmas present for Arch. How are your cats?"

"They're great! Koko's getting smarter all the time. He opens doors, turns light on and off, and he's learning to type."

"You're kidding."

"He rubs his jaw against the levers and flips the carriage or resets margins—not always at the most opportune time."

"He's cleaning his teeth," Rosie explained. "Our vet says that's how cats try to clean their teeth. You should take Koko to the dentist. Our gray tabby just had a dental prophylaxis. . . . Say, have you got any tin? I want to buy something for Arch."

She found a tin knife box, and Qwilleran—torn between two loyalties—guiltily knocked two dollars off Mrs. Cobb's asking price.

Rosie said, "I thought your story on the auction was great!"

"The story behind the story is better."

"What's that? Arch didn't tell me. He never tells me anything."

Qwilleran reconstructed the night of Andy's accident. "I can't believe," he said, "that Andy simply missed his footing and fell. He'd have to have been an acrobat to land on the finial the way he did. There were customers coming to look at a chandelier that night. If he was in the process of getting it down off the ceiling, it would mean they had already okayed it; in other words, they were there when he fell! . . . It doesn't click. I don't think they ever got in the store. I think the whole accident was staged, and Andy was dead when the customers arrived."

As he talked, Rosie's eyes had been growing wider and wider. "Qwill, I think Arch and I . . . I think we might have been the customers! When did it happen?"

"Middle of October. The sixteenth, to be exact."

"We wanted to get this chandelier installed before our Halloween party, but I didn't want to buy it without Arch seeing it. He came home to dinner, and then we drove back to Junktown. Andy was going to open up especially for us. But when we got there, the store was locked up, and no one was in sight. In the meantime I noticed a chandelier in the Cobbs' window that looked good, so we bought that one instead."

"Were the Cobbs open at that late hour?"

"No, but we saw someone going up the steps and asked him if the Cobbs would mind coming down to show us the fixture. He went upstairs and got Mrs. Cobb, and we bought it. It was a couple of weeks later that one of my junking friends told me about Andy's accident, and I never connected—"

"Who was the man who was going up the Cobbs' front steps?"

"He's a dealer himself. He has the Bit o' Junk shop. It really worked out better for us, because the fixture we bought from Mrs. Cobb was painted tin, and I realized afterwards that Andy's brass chandelier would have been too formal for our dining room."

"Did you say brass?"

"Yes. Sort of Williamsburg."

"Not glass? Not a chandelier with five crystal arms?"

"Oh, no! Crystal would be much too dressy for our house."

That was when Qwilleran kissed Rosie Riker.

Later in the afternoon he made a few additional entries in the log:

—Sold turkey platter, $75.

—Customer broke goblet. Collected $4.50. Showed no mercy.

—Sold apple peeler to make into a lamp, $12.

—Sold bronze grille from Garrick Theatre, $45.

—Photographer sat in banister-back chair. *Fluxion* will pay for damage.

—SOLD ROLL-TOP DESK, $750!

The woman who came bursting into the shop, asking for a roll-top desk, was not an experienced junker. Qwilleran could tell that by her enthusiasm and her smart clothes.

"The man next door told me you have a roll-top desk," she announced breathlessly, "and I must have one before Christmas."

"The one we have is in use," said Qwilleran, "and the user would be extremely reluctant to part with it."

"I don't care what it costs," she said. "I've got to have it for my husband's Christmas gift. I'll write you a check, and my driver will pick it up in the morning."

Qwilleran felt pleased with himself that evening. He had personally taken in almost $1,000 for Mrs. Cobb. He had gleaned information from Rosie Riker that reinforced his theory about the finial incident. And he had broached an idea to the managing editor of the *Daily Fluxion* that had made a big impression; it if proved to be workable—and the boss felt that it might—it would solve a lot of problems for a lot of people.

After dinner Qwilleran was removing his belongings from the pigeonholes of the roll-top desk when he heard a heavy tread coming up the stairs. He opened his door and hailed his neighbor. Ben was still wearing his Santa Claus disguise.

"Ben, what's a roll-top desk worth?" Qwilleran asked. "There's no price tag on the one I'm using, and I sold it for seven hundred and fifty, chair included."

"Oh, excellent swindle!" said the dealer. "Sir, you

should be in the business." He trudged toward his apartment, then turned around and resolutely trudged back. "Will you join me in a drop of brandy and a crumb of rare cheese?"

"I'll go for some of that cheese," Qwilleran said. He had just finished an unsatisfactory dinner of canned stew.

His host moved a copper wash boiler from the seat of a Victorian sofa, leaving an oval silhouette in the dust on the black horsehair, and the newsman sat on the clean spot and surveyed the appointments of the room: a bust of Hiawatha, a wooden plane propellor, empty picture frames, a wicker baby carriage, a leather pail labeled FIRE, a wooden washboard, a wigless doll.

Ben brought Qwilleran some cheese and crackers on a plate decorated with an advertisement for an 1870 patent medicine that relieved itching. Then he lowered himself with a groan into a creaking chair of mildewed wicker. "We are faint," he said. "Our gashes cry for help." He drank fastidiously from a cracked teacup.

Ben had removed his white beard, and now he looked absurd with rouged nose and cheeks, pale jowls, and powdered artificial eyebrows.

Qwilleran said, "I've been in Junktown a week now, and frankly I don't know how you dealers make a living."

"We muddle through. We muddle through."

"Where do you acquire your goods? Where does it all come from?"

Ben waved a hand at the sculptured head of an angel, minus nose. "Behold! A repulsive little gem from the façade of the Garrick Theatre. Genuine stone, with the original bird droppings." He waved toward a discolored washbowl and pitcher. "A treasure from Mount Vernon, with the original soap scum."

For half an hour Qwilleran plied his host with questions, receiving flowery answers with no information whatever. At last he prepared to leave, and as he glanced at a few stray cracker crumbs on the seat of the black horsehair sofa, he saw something else that alerted him—a stiff blond hair. He casually picked it up.

Back in his own apartment he examined the hair under a lamp. There was no doubt what it was— three inches long, slightly curved, tapering at one end.

He went to the telephone and dialed a number.

"Mary," he said, "I've made a discovery. Do you want to see something interesting? Put on your coat and run over here."

Then he turned to the cats, who were lounging contentedly on their gilded chairs.

"Okay, you guys!" he said. "What do you know about this?"

Koko scratched his left ear with his hind foot, and Yum Yum licked her right shoulder.

TWENTY

Qwilleran heard Ben Nicholas leave the house, and shortly afterward the downstairs buzzer sounded, and Mary Duckworth arrived with a fur parka thrown over a skyblue corduroy jumpsuit.

She examined the stiff blond hair.

"Know what it is?" Qwilleran asked.

"A bristle. From some kind of brush."

"It's a whisker," he corrected her, "from some kind of cat. I found it on Ben's living room sofa. Either my two rascals have found a way to get into the apartment next door, or the spirit of Mathilda Spencer is getting pretty cheeky."

Mary examined the cat whisker. "It's mottled— white and gray."

"It obviously belongs to Yum Yum. Koko's are pure white."

"Have you any idea how they could get through the wall?"

Qwilleran beckoned her to follow as he led the way to the dressing room. "I've checked out the bathroom. The wall is solid tile. The only other possibility is in here—behind these bookshelves."

Koko followed them into the dressing room and rubbed his jaw ardently against the books on the lower shelf.

"Beautiful bindings!" Mary said. "Mrs. Cobb could sell these to decorators for several dollars apiece."

There was a yowl from Koko, but it was a muffled yowl, and Qwilleran looked down in time to see a tail tip disappearing between two volumes—in precisely the spot where he had removed the bound copies of *The Liberator*.

"Koko, come out!" he ordered. "It's dusty back there."

"Yow!" came the faint reply.

Mary said, "He sounds as if he's down a deep well."

The man attacked the bookshelf with both hands, pulling out volumes and tossing them on the floor. "Bring the flashlight, Mary. It's on the desk."

He flashed the light toward the back wall, and its beamed picked up an expanse of paneling similar to the fireplace wall in the living room—narrow planks with beveled edges.

"Solid," said Qwilleran. "Let's clear more shelves . . . Ouch!"

"Careful! Don't twist your knee, Qwill. Let me do it."

Mary got down on her hands and knees and peered under a low shelf. "Qwill, there's an opening in the wall, sure enough."

"How big?"

"It looks as if a single board is missing."

"Can you see what's beyond? Take the flashlight."

"There's another wall—about two feet back. It makes a narrow compartment—"

"Mary, do you think . . . ?"

"Qwill, could this be . . . ?"

The idea occurred to them both, simultaneously.

"An Underground Railway station," Qwilleran said.

"Exactly!" she said. "William Towne Spencer built this house."

"Many abolitionists—"

"Built secret rooms—yes!"

"To hide runaway slaves."

Mary ducked her head under the shelf again. "It slides!" she called over her shoulder. "The whole panel is a sliding door. There's a robe in here." She pulled out twelve feet of white cord. "And a toothbrush!"

"Yow!" said Koko, making a sudden appearance

in the beam of the flashlight. He stepped out from his hideaway and staggered a little as he gave a delicate shudder.

"Close the panel," Qwilleran directed. "Can you close it?"

"All but half an inch. It seems to be warped."

"I'll bet Koko opened the panel with his claws, and Yum Yum followed him through. She's the one who did the fetching and carrying. . . . Well, that solves one mystery. How about a cup of coffee?"

"Thanks, no. I must go home. I'm wrapping Christmas presents." Mary stopped short. "You've been emptying your desk! Are you moving out?"

"Only the desk is moving. I sold it this afternoon for seven hundred and fifty dollars."

"Qwill, you didn't! It's worth two hundred dollars at most."

He showed her the log of his afternoon session in The Junkery. "Not bad for a greenhorn, is it?"

"Who is this woman who wanted Sheffield candlesticks?" Mary asked, as she scanned the report. "You should have sent her to me. . . . And who was asking for horse brasses? No one buys horse brasses any more."

"What are they?"

"Brass medallions for decorating harnesses. The English used to use them as good luck tokens. . . . Who's the customer who got kissed? That's a devious way to sell a tin knife box."

"She's the wife of our feature editor," Qwilleran said. "By the way, I've brought a present for Arch

Riker—just a joke. Would you gift-wrap it for me?"
He handed Mary the rusty tobacco tin.

"I hope," she said, reading the price tag inside the cover, "that the Weird Sisters didn't charge you ten dollars for this."

"Ten dollars?" Qwilleran felt an uncomfortable sensation on his upper lip. "They were asking ten, but they gave it to me for five."

"That's not bad. Most shops get seven-fifty."

Gulping his chagrin, Qwilleran escorted her down the stairs, and as they passed Ben's open door he asked, "Does the Bit o' Junk do a good business?"

"Not particularly," she replied. "Ben is too lazy to go out looking for things, so his turnover is slow."

"He took me to The Lion's Tail last night, and he was throwing money around as if he had his own printing press."

Mary shrugged. "He must have had a windfall. Once a year a dealer can count on a windfall—like selling a roll-top desk for seven hundred and fifty dollars. That's one of the great truths of the antique business."

"By the way," Qwilleran said, "we went scrounging at the Garrick last night, but all that was left was a crest on one of the boxes, and I almost broke my neck trying to get it."

"Ben should have warned you. That box has been unsafe for years."

"How do you know?"

"The city engineers condemned it in the 1940s

and ordered it padlocked. It's called the Ghost Box."

"Do you think Ben knew about it?"

"Everyone knows about it," Mary said. "That's why the crest was never taken. Even Russ Patch refused to risk it, and he's a daredevil."

After Qwilleran had watched her return to her own house, he climbed the stairs pensively. At the top of the flight the cats were waiting for him in identical poses, sitting tall with brown tails arranged in matching curves. One inch of tail tip lifted inquiringly.

"You scoundrels!" Qwilleran said. "I suppose you've been having a whale of a time, coming and going through the walls like a couple of apparitions."

Koko stropped his jaw on the newel post, his tiny ivory tusks clicking against the ancient mahogany.

"Want to go and have your teeth cleaned?" the man asked him. "After Christmas I'll take you to a cat dentist."

Koko rubbed the back of his head on the newel post—an ingratiating gesture.

"Don't pretend innocence. You don't fool me for a minute." Qwilleran roughed up the sleek fur along the cat's fluid backbone. "What else have you been doing behind my back? What are you planning to do next?"

That was Wednesday night. Thursday morning Qwilleran got his answer.

Just before daylight he turned in his bed and

found his nose buried in fur. Yum Yum was sharing
his pillow. Her fur smelled clean. Qwilleran's mind
went back forty-odd years to a sunny backyard with
laundry flapping on the clothesline. The clean wash
smelled like sunshine and fresh air, and that was the
fragrance of this small animal's coat.

From the kitchen came a familiar sound:
"Yawwck!" It was Koko's good-morning yowl com-
bined with a wake-up yawn, and it was followed by
two thumps as the cat jumped down from refrigerator to counter to floor. When he walked into the living room, he stopped in the middle of the carpet and
pushed his forelegs forward, his hind quarters sky-
ward, in an elongated stretch. After that he stretched
a hind leg—just the left one—very carefully. Then he
approached the swan bed and ordered breakfast in
clarion tones.

The man made no move to get out of bed but
reached out a teasing hand. Koko sidestepped it and
rubbed his brown mask against the corner of the
bed. He crossed the room and rubbed the leg of the
book cupboard. He walked to the Morris chair and
stropped his jaw on its square corners.

"Just what do you think you're accomplishing?"
Qwilleran asked.

Koko ambled to the pot-bellied stove and looked
it over, then selected the latch of the ashpit door and
ground his jaw against it. He scraped the left side of
his jaw; he scraped the right side. And the shallow
door clicked and swung ajar. The door opened only

a hair's-breadth, but Koko pried it farther with an inquisitive paw.

In a split second Qwilleran was out of bed and bending over the ashpit. It was full of papers—type-written sheets—a stack of them two inches thick, neatly bound in gray folders. They had been typed on a machine with a loose E—a faulty letter that jumped above the line.

TWENTY-ONE

In the gray-white morning light of the day before the day before Christmas, Qwilleran started to read Andy's novel. The questionable heroine of the story was a scatterbrained prattler who was planning to spike her alcoholic husband's highball with carbon tetrachloride in order to be free to marry another man of great sexual prowess.

He had read six chapters when a uniformed chauffeur and two truckers arrived to remove the roll-top desk, and after that it was time to shave and dress and go downtown. He put the manuscript back in the ashpit reluctantly.

At the *Fluxion* office Qwilleran's session with the managing editor lasted longer than either of them had anticipated. In fact, it stretched into a lengthy lunch date with some important executives in a private dining room at the Press Club, and when the newsman returned to Junktown in the late afternoon, he was jubilant.

His knee, much improved, permitted him to bolt up the front steps of the Cobb mansion two at a time, but when he let himself into the entrance hall, he slowed down. The Cobb Junkery was open, and Iris was there, moving in a daze, passing a dustrag over the arms of a Boston rocker.

"I didn't expect you so soon," he said.

"I thought I ought to open the shop," she replied in a dreary voice. "There might be some follow-up business after the Block Party, and goodness knows I need the money. Dennis—my son—came back with me."

"We sold some merchandise for you yesterday," Qwilleran said. "I hated to let my desk go, but a woman was willing to pay seven hundred and fifty dollars for it."

Iris exhibited more gratitude than surprise.

"And incidentally, were you saving any old radios for Hollis Prantz?" he asked.

"Old radios? No, we wouldn't have anything like that."

That evening Qwilleran finished reading Andy's novel. It was just as he expected. The characters included a philandering husband, a voluptuous di-

vorcée, a poor little rich girl operating a swanky antique shop incognito, and—in the later chapters—a
retired schoolteacher who was naive to the point of
stupidity. For good measure Andy had also introduced a gambling racketeer, a nymphet, a dope
pusher, a sodomite, a crooked politician, and a retired cop who appeared to be the mouthpiece for the
author's highminded platitudes.

Why, Qwilleran asked himself, had Andy hidden
his manuscript in the ashpit of a pot-bellied stove?

At one point his reading was interrupted by a
knock on his door, and a clean-cut young man
wearing a white shirt and bowtie introduced himself
as Iris's son.

"My mother says you need a desk," he said. "If
you'll give me an assist, we can bring the one from
her apartment."

"The apothecary desk? I don't want to deprive
her—"

"She says she doesn't need it."

"How's your mother feeling?"

"Rough! She took a pill and went to bed early."

They carried the desk across the hall, and a chair
to go with it—a Windsor with thick slab seat and
delicate spindle back—and Qwilleran asked Dennis
to help him hoist the Mackintosh coat of arms to
the mantel, replacing the portrait of the sour-faced
kill-joy.

Then Qwilleran plunged once more into Andy's
novel. He had read worse books, but not many.
Andy had no ear for dialogue and no compassion

for his characters. What fascinated the newsman, however, was the narcotics operation. One of the antique dealers in the story dispensed marijuana as well as mahogany sideboards and Meissen ewers. Whenever a customer walked into his shop and asked for a Quimper teapot, he was actually in the market for "tea."

After four hundred pages of jumping E's, Qwilleran's eyelids were heavy and his eyeballs were aching. He leaned his head back in the Morris chair and closed his eyes. Quimper teapots! He had never heard of a Quimper teapot, but there were many things he had not heard of before coming to Junktown: Sussex pigs . . . piggins, noggins and firkins . . . horse brasses.

Horse brasses! Qwilleran's moustache danced, and he reproved it with his knuckles. No one buys horse brasses any more, Mary had said. And yet— twice during his short stay in Junktown, he had heard a request for this useless brass ornament.

The first inquiry had been at the Bit o' Junk shop, and Ben had been inclined to dismiss the customer curtly. Yesterday the same inquiry was made at The Junkery. The two buildings were adjacent, and similar in design.

Qwilleran combed his moustache to subdue his excitement and devised a plan for the next morning. The twenty-fourth of December was going to be a busy day: the big party in the evening, another appointment with the managing editor in the afternoon, lunch with Arch Riker at the Press Club, and in the morning—a tactical maneuver that might fill in another blank in the Junktown puzzle.

The next day Qwilleran was waked before dawn by flashing lights. Koko was standing on the bed, rubbing his teeth with satisfaction on the wall switch and turning the lamps on and off.

The man got up, opened a can of corned beef for the cats, shaved and dressed. As soon as he thought the Dispatch Desk was open, he telephoned and asked them to send a messenger at eleven thirty—no later and no earlier.

"Send me the skinniest and shabbiest one you've got," he told the dispatch clerk. "Preferably one with a bad cold or an acute sinus infection."

While waiting for the accomplice to arrive, Qwilleran moved his paper and pencils, clips and gluepot into the apothecary desk. In one of the drawers he found Iris Cobb's tape recorder and returned it to her.

"I don't want it," she said with a sickly attempt at a smile. "I don't even want to look at it. Maybe you can use it in your work."

The youth who arrived from the Dispatch Office was unkempt, undernourished and red-eyed. Most of the *Fluxion* messengers fitted such a description, but this one was superlative.

"Yikes!" the boy said when he saw the newsman's apartment. "Do you pay rent for this pad, or does the *Flux* pay you to live here?"

"Don't editorialize," Qwilleran said, reaching for

his wallet. "Just do what I say. Here's ten bucks. Go next door—"

"Lookit them crazy cats! Do they bite?"

"Only *Fluxion* messengers. . . . Now listen carefully. Go to the antique shop called Bit o' Junk and ask if the man has any horse brasses."

"Horse *what?*"

"The man who runs the place is crazy, so don't be surprised at anything he does or says. And don't let him know that you know me—or that you work for the *Flux*. Just ask if he has any horse brasses and show him your money. Then bring me whatever he gives you."

"Horse brasses! You gotta be kiddin'."

"Don't go straight there. Hang around on the corner a few minutes before you approach the Bit o' Junk. . . . And try not to look too intelligent!" Qwilleran called after the departing messenger, as an unnecessary afterthought.

Then he paced the floor in suspense. When a cat jumped on the desk and presented an arched back at a convenient level for stroking, the man stroked it absently.

In fifteen minutes the messenger returned. He said, "Ten bucks for this thing? You gotta be nuts!"

"I guess you're right," said Qwilleran meekly, as he examined the brass medallion the boy handed him.

It was a setback, but the fluttering sensation in his moustache told Qwilleran that he was on the right track, and he refused to be discouraged.

At noon he met Arch Riker at the Press Club and presented him with the tobacco tin, gift-wrapped in a page from an 1864 Harper's Weekly.

"It's great!" the feature editor said. "But you shouldn't have spent so much, Qwill. Hell, I didn't buy you anything, but I'll pop for lunch."

In the afternoon Qwilleran spent a satisfactory hour with the managing editor, and then joined the Women's Department for pink lemonade and Christmas cookies, and later turned up at an impromptu celebration in the Photo Lab, where he was the only sober guest, and eventually went home.

He had three hours before his date with Mary. He went to the ashpit and once more read the chapter in Andy's novel that dealt with the dope pusher.

At five o'clock he dashed out and picked up the better of his two suits from Junktown's dry cleaning establishment that specialized in quick service. There was a red tag on his garment.

"You musta left something in the pocket," the clerk said, and she rummaged through a drawer until she found an envelope with his name on it.

When Qwilleran noted the contents, he said, "Thanks! Thanks very much! Have a Christmas drink on me," and he left a dollar tip.

"It was the tape measure. Mary's silver tape measure and a piece of folded paper.

Fingering the smooth silver case, he returned to his apartment and looked out his back window. The early winter dusk was doing its best to make the junk in the backyard look more bedraggled than ever. The two station wagons were there, backed in from the alley—one gray and one tan.

Access to the backyard was apparently through the Cobb shop, and Qwilleran preferred to avoid Iris, so he went out the front door, around the corner and in through the alley. After a glance at the back windows of nearby houses, he measured the gray wagon. It was exactly as he had guessed; the dimensions tallied with the notations on the scrap of paper.

And as he walked around the decrepit vehicle he noted something else that checked; Ben's wagon had a left front fender missing.

Qwilleran knew exactly what he wanted to do now. After buying a pint of the best brandy at Lombardo's, he ran up the steps to the Bit o' Junk shop. The front door was open, but Ben's store was locked up and dark.

He stopped at The Junkery. "Happen to know where Ben is?" he asked Iris. "I'd like to extend the hospitality of the season."

"He must be at Children's Hospital," Iris said. "He goes there every Christmas to play Santa."

Upstairs the cats were waiting. Both were sitting tall in the middle of the floor, with the attentive attitude that meant, "We have a message to communicate." They were staring. Yum Yum was staring into middle distance with her crossed eyes, but she was staring hard. Koko stared at a certain point in the center of Qwilleran's forehead, and he was staring so intently that his body swayed with an inner tension.

This was not the dinner message, Qwilleran knew. This was something more important. "What is it?" he asked the cats. "What are you trying to tell me?"

Koko turned his head. He looked at a small shiny object on the floor near the bookcase.

"What's that?" Qwilleran gasped, although he needed no answer. He knew what it was.

He picked up the scrap of silvery paper and took it to the desk. He turned on the lamp. At first glance the foil looked like a gum wrapper that had been stepped on, but he knew better. It was a neat rectangle, as wide as a pencil, and as thin as a razorblade.

As he started to open the packet, Koko jumped to the desk to watch. With dainty brown feet the cat stepped over pencils, paper clips, ashtray, tobacco pouch, and tape measure, and then he stepped precisely on the green button of Iris's portable tape recorder.

"Hawnnk . . . ssss . . . hawnnk . . . ssss . . ."

Qwilleran hit the red button of the machine and silenced the unpleasant noise. As he did so, he became aware of heavy footsteps in the hall.

Santa Claus was lumbering up the stairs, pulling on the handrail for assistance.

"Come in and toast the season," Qwilleran invited. "I've got a good bottle of brandy."

"Worthy gentleman, I'll do that!" Ben said.

He shuffled into Qwilleran's quarters in his big black boots cuffed with imitation fur. His eyes were glazed, his breath was strong; he had not come directly from Children's Hospital.

"Ho ho ho!" he said in hearty greeting when he spied the two cats.

Yum Yum flew to the top of the book cupboard, but Koko stood his ground and glared at the visitor.

"Merr-r-r-y Christmas!" boomed the Santa Claus voice.

Koko's backbone bristled. He arched his back and bushed his tail. With ears laid back and fangs bared, he hissed. Then Koko jumped to the desk and continued to watch the proceedings—with disapproval in the angle of his ears and the tilt of his whiskers. From his perch he could survey the Morris chair, where Qwilleran sat drinking coffee, and the rocker, where Santa Claus was sipping brandy. He also had a good view of the tea table, which held a plate of smoked oysters.

At length Qwilleran said, "Let's drink to our old friend Cobb, wherever he is!"

Ben waved his glass. "To the perfidious wretch!"

"You mean you weren't an admirer of our late landlord?"

"Fair is foul, and foul is fair," said the old actor.

"I'd like to know what happened that night at the Ellsworth house. Did Cobb have a heart attack, or did he slip on the stairs? The snow could have caked on his boots, you now. It was snowing that night, wasn't it?"

There was no confirmation from Ben, whose rouged nose was deep in his brandy glass.

"I mean, sometime after midnight," Qwilleran persisted. "Do you remember? Wasn't it snowing? Were you out that night?"

"Oh, it snowed and it blowed . . . it blew and it snew," said Ben with appropriate grimaces and gestures.

"I went to the Ellsworth house the next day, and there was a bare patch under Cobb's car, indicating that it was snowing while he was stripping the house. The funny thing is: another car had been there at the same time. It left its outline on the ice, and from the shape of the impression, I would guess the second car had a fender missing." Qwilleran paused and watched Ben's face.

"Mischief, thou are afoot!" said Ben, looking mysterious.

Qwilleran tried other approaches to no avail. The old actor was a better actor than he. The newsman kept an eye on his watch; he had to shave and dress before calling for Mary.

He made one more attempt. "I wonder if it's true," he said, "that Ellsworth had some dough hidden—"

He was interrupted by a noise from the desk. "Hawnnk . . . ssss . . . hawnnk . . ."

"Koko! Scram!" he yelled, and the cat jumped to the floor and up on the mantel, almost in a single swoop. "If it's true that the old house had some hidden treasure," Qwilleran continued, "perhaps Cobb got his hands on it—"

The tape recorder went on: "Hawnnk . . . sssss . . . ppphlat!"

"And perhaps someone came along and gave him a shove." Qwilleran was lounging casually in his chair but watching Ben sharply, and he thought he detected a wavering eye—a glance that was not in the actor's script. "Someone might have shoved him down the stairs and grabbed the loot . . ."

"Hawnnk . . . ppphlat!" said the recorder. Then "Grrrummph! Whazzat? Whatcha doin'?" There followed the murmur of blank tape. then: "Wool over my eyes, you old fool. . . . Know what you're up to. . . . Think you can get away with anything. . . . Over my dead body!"

It was Cobb's recorded voice, and Qwilleran sat up straight.

The tape said, "Those creeps comin' in here. . . . Horse brasses, my eye! . . . Know where you get your deliveries. . . . You! Scroungin' at the Garrick! That's a laugh!"

Ben dropped his glass of brandy and heaved himself out of the rocker.

"No!" yelled Qwilleran, erupting from the Morris chair and leaping toward the desk. "I've got to hear this!"

The tape said, "Me marchin' on the picket line, a lousy three bucks an hour, and you get ten for a deck . . ."

The newsman stared at the machine with incredulity and triumph.

The tape said, "Not any more, you don't. . . . You're gonna cut me in, Ben Baby. . . ."

There was a flash of red in the room. Qwilleran saw it from the corner of his eye. It moved toward the fireplace, and the newsman spun around in time to see Ben reaching for the poker. Then a big black Santa Claus boot kicked out, and the tea table went flying across the room.

Qwilleran reached for the desk chair, without taking his eyes from the red suit. He grabbed the chair roughly by its back, but all he got was a handful of spindles; the back came off in his hand.

For an instant the two men were face to face— Ben bracing himself on the hearth and brandishing the poker, Qwilleran holding a few useless dowels. And then—the iron thing shot forward. It skidded off the mantel, catching Ben in the neck. As the poker flew through the air, Qwilleran ducked, skidded on an oyster, and went down on his right knee with a thud.

The scene of action froze in a tableau: Santa Claus on the floor, flattened by the Mackintosh coat of arms; Qwilleran on his knees; Koko bending over a smoked oyster.

After the police had taken Ben away, and while Iris and Dennis were helping to straighten up the room, the telephone rang, and Qwilleran walked slowly and painfully to the desk.

"What's the matter, Qwill?" asked Mary's anxious voice. "I just heard the siren and saw them taking Ben away in the police car. "What's wrong?"

Qwilleran moaned. "Everything! Including my knee."

"You've hurt it again?"

"It's the *other* knee. I'm immobilized. I don't know what to do about the party."

"We can have the party at your place, but what about Ben?"

"I'll explain when you get here."

She came wearing blue chiffon and bearing Christmas gifts. "What on earth has happened to Ben—and your knee?" she demanded.

"We caught a murderer here tonight," Qwilleran said. "With the aid of your tape measure I placed Ben at the scene of Cobb's accident."

"I can't believe it! Did he admit he killed C.C.?"

"Not in so many words. He merely gave his landlord Godspeed with an auspicious push."

"Was it true about buried treasure at the Ellsworth house?"

"No, it was a case of blackmail. Ben was pushing heroin, Mary. He met his supplier at the abandoned theatre and bagged the stuff in five-grain decks."

"How did you find out?"

"The cats brought me a deck from Ben's apartment, and Andy's novel gave me another tip. The junkies would identify themselves in Ben's shop by asking for horse brasses."

"That was a clever arrangement."

"But the addicts sometimes wandered into the wrong shop, and Cobb apparently caught on. And here's the incredible part of the story: When Cobb was demanding a cut of Ben's profits, the complete conversation was recorded on tape! I think Koko flipped the switch on Iris's tape recorder when Cobb was trying to make his deal with Ben."

"What a fantastic coincidence!"

"Fantastic, yes! But if you knew Koko, you wouldn't be too sure it was coincidental. It must have happened Sunday morning when Iris was at church and I was at the drugstore."

"Koko, you're a hero!" Mary said to the cat, who was now taking his lordly ease on the daybed. "And you're going to have a reward. Pressed duck!" She turned to Qwilleran. "I took the liberty of ordering dinner. It's being sent over from the Toledo Restaurant. I hope you like oysters Rockefeller and pressed duck and Chateaubriand and French Strawberries."

"But no more rich food for the cats," he said. "They've eaten a whole can of smoked oysters, and I'm afraid they'll be sick." He looked at Koko with speculation and added, "There's one thing we'll never know. How did the Mackintosh coat of arms happen to slide off the mantel at the strategic moment? Just as Ben raised the poker to beat my brains out, that chunk of iron delivered a karate chop."

He gazed at Koko with conjecture and admiration, and the cat rolled over and licked the pale fur on his stomach.

The telephone rang. "Probably our police reporter," Qwilleran said. "I asked him to call me when the police had more details."

He went limping to the desk.

"Yes, Lodge. Any developments? . . . That's what I guessed. . . . How did he find out? . . . He had his finger on everything, that boy! . . . Yes, I've met the guy. . . . No, I won't mention it."

When the newsman hung up, he refrained from telling Mary that the Narcotics Squad had been watching Junktown for three months and that Hollis Prantz was an undercover agent. Nor did he tell her immediately about Ben's complete confession.

Dinner arrived from the city's most expensive restaurant—in chafing dishes and under silver covers and on beds of crushed ice—and Mary presented her Christmas gifts: a case of canned lobster for the cats and a pair of Scottish brass candlesticks for Qwilleran.

"I have a surprise for you, too," he told her, "but first you must hear some painful truths. Andy's death was not accidental. He was Ben's first victim."

"But why? Why?"

"Ben was afraid Andy would turn him in. Both Andy and Cobb had learned about Ben's sideline. Our actor friend was in danger of losing the thing he valued most in the world—an audience—even though he had to buy their applause. On the night of October sixteenth, after he saw Cobb leave Andy's shop, he slipped in and staged the so-called accident."

"And did he kill that poor man in the alley?"

"No. Ben declined to take bows for that one. The police were right that time. One out of three."

Mary caught her breath. "But what will happen now? There will be a trial! I'll have to testify!"

"Don't be alarmed," he said. "Everything's arranged so that you can come out of hiding. For the last two days I've been meeting with *Fluxion* executives and the mayor's aides and your father. I've proposed an idea—"

"My father!"

"Not a bad guy—your dad. The city is going to establish a Landmarks Preservation Committee, prompted by the *Fluxion* and underwritten by your father's bank as a public service. He's agreed to act as honorary chairman. But *you* are going to spearhead the program."

"I?"

"Yes, you! It's time you started putting your knowledge and enthusiasm to work. And here's something else: scrounging is going to be legalized. All you need is a permit and—"

"Qwill, did you do all this for Junktown?"

"No. Mostly for you," he said. "And if you make this contribution to the success of Junktown, I don't think you'll be bothered by those crank calls any more. Someone wanted to scare you—to chase you out of the neighborhood. I think I know who, but the less said the better."

Mary's expression of delight and gratitude was all the Christmas that Qwilleran needed—better, much better, than the brass candlesticks—better, almost, than the $1,000 prize he was sure of winning.

His satisfaction was short-lived, however. The

girl's eyes clouded, and she swallowed hard. "If only Andy were here," she mourned. "How he would—"

"Koko!" shouted Qwilleran. "Get away from that wall!"

Koko was standing on the daybed and sharpening his claws on Andy's carefully pasted wall covering.

"He's been working on that blasted wall ever since we moved in," the man said. "The corners are beginning to curl up."

Mary looked across the room, blinking her eyes emotionally. Then she stood up quickly and walked to the daybed. Koko scampered away.

"Qwill," she said, "there's something else here." She pulled at one of the curled corners, and a page of *Don Quixote* started to peel off.

Qwilleran hobbled across the room and joined her on the daybed.

"There's something pasted underneath this page," she said, peeling it slowly and carefully.

"Greenbacks!"

"Money!"

Under the page that Mary was pulling off there were three hundred-dollar bills.

Qwilleran peeled a page of Samuel Pepys and found three more. "Iris told me Andy had used peelable paste, and now we know why!"

"Where did Andy get these?" Mary cried. "He didn't make this kind of money! Any profit he made went right back into antiques." She peeled off another page. "This whole wall is papered with currency! How did Andy—"

"Maybe he had a sideline," said Qwilleran. "Do you suppose he did business with Papa Popopopoulos?"

"I can't believe it!" Mary said. "Andy was so . . . He was so . . . Why would he *hide* it like this?"

"The usual reason," Qwilleran said, clearing his throat diplomatically, "has to do with unreported income."

He said it as gently as he could, but Mary collapsed in tears. He put his arms around her and comforted her, and she was willing to be comforted.

Neither of them noticed Koko as he rose weightlessly to the swanlike daybed. Standing on his hind feet he rubbed his jaw against the carved wood. He stretched his neck and rubbed the nearby doorjamb. He rubbed against the light switch, and the apartment was thrown into darkness.

In the moments that followed, the pair on the daybed were blissfully unaware of two pale apparitions hovering over the dinner table in the vicinity of the pressed duck.

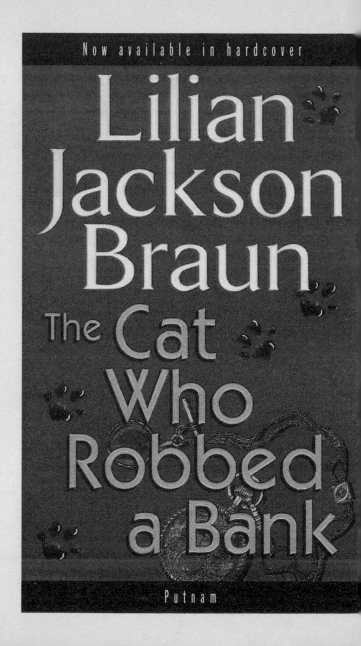

Now available in hardcover

Lilian Jackson Braun

The Cat Who Robbed a Bank

Putnam